Moonlight Express

Geoff Barlow

This is a work of fiction. Besides accurate historical places, facts and information, the individuals, characters and corporations found within are purely fictional.

Strictly Literary,
81 Hoff Street,
Mount Gravatt East
www.strictlyliterary.com
Cell phone: 0413 004 138

First published by Strictly Literary, Australia, © 2012.

ISBN: 978-0-9870865-8-7 (pbk)

Typeset in 13/15 Garamond by Strictly Literary
Cover image © Emma Barlow, used under licence.
Worldwide distribution: visit Lulu
http://www.lulu.com/spotlight/strictlyliterary

What the hammer? What the chain?
In what furnace was thy brain?
What the anvil? What dread grasp
Dare its deadly terrors clasp?

William Blake

Foreword

IT'S MORE THAN 30 years since the events in this narrative took place, so I suppose the government won't be too worried about the release of the information. I know all the major players in the story are happy for everything to be brought out into the open – the honest ones are, at least, and the opinion of the others shouldn't really matter.

The dates and times should be fairly accurate, and the report has largely been set out in sequence, give or take some discrepancies due to international time zones. The reason the whole business should be recorded, I think, is as a cautionary tale, and also as a tribute to the actions of some quite remarkable people. This is how one young woman, with a few friends, set out to make a difference: they all looked danger right in the face, and tried their hardest to put a few things right.

Chapter One
Saturday 25th June 1977

IT HAD BEEN one of those delicious, almost intoxicating, mid-year days in the foothills of the Dividing Range – an early frost, which left the air sparkling clear as the soft winter sun vaulted through a pastel blue sky; then a mellow, amber afternoon light that deepened swiftly, till at last a dusty orange glow mantled the western ridges, and a purple dusk cloaked the rich alluvial valleys.

For most of the day a bright yellow Holden Monaro had mirrored the course of the sun, its two young occupants at one with the mood and spirit of the season. They had roamed through the morning throngs of the village markets, strolled hand in hand beside quiet creeks, and picnicked beside a glistening lake, its surface alive with the roar of power boats and a riot of sail. They had watched the elegant billows of skydivers falling among the lengthening shadows of a grassy airfield, and eaten hamburgers at an ancient roadhouse while the twilight fell around the outdoor tables.

And now, as the wash of a brilliant moon flooded over the fields of potatoes and lucerne, the couple in the Monaro trundled down little used laneways, questing for places where the light was dimmer and the only other human sounds were the punk rock emissions from the car radio. The driver down-shifted and the big V8 rumbled deeply while he nosed the car up a steep embankment. The engine note changed to a steady pulsing idle as the ground levelled off, then fell silent as the young man flicked the key.

'Warren!' The girl in the passenger seat was about twenty years of age, with a wedge-shaped thatch of blonde hair, a zippered coat, blue jeans and sheepskin boots. 'Do you realise you've gone and bloody well parked across a railway track? This is your idea of a quiet romantic spot?' The tone might have been serious, but the grin on the pretty face suggested otherwise.

'No worries, Angie.' Warren Schultz was a tall, slim youth with long dark hair and a face that seemed creased in a permanent smile. He was twenty-four but looked younger, and despite the coolness of the evening he wore only a tee shirt, shorts and rubber thongs. 'This was the old branch line out to Rinehart's Ridge – hasn't been used since the war, the oldies reckon. I doubt if the railway big knobs are suddenly gonna start sendin' trains from Ipswich up to Toowoomba via some new route, do you?'

'Via some *old* route, don't you mean?' Angela Reimann was still in a somewhat corrective mood, though her grin was now almost as wide as her boyfriend's.

'Yeah, s'pose so.' Warren's voice was softer, his

face much closer. To the dulcet tones of a Swedish pop group, the duo relaxed into each other's arms, creatures of the soft moonlight, the wispy shadows of trees, the music – until Angela's attention was suddenly caught by a blade of baleful yellow light, scything through the undergrowth.

'Warren – what's that?' The girl's voice was a whisper.

'What's what?'

'You reckon there might be another car out here?'

'Nah, why?'

'Well, what's that ... light?' The strain was too much for Angela. She sat bolt upright, eyes darting over Warren's shoulder – and saw the face of a monster from a vanished age, charging straight at them.

'TRAI-!' The girl's scream was drowned out by the shriek of a steam whistle, the clatter of metal wheels, and the clanking heart of the vast leviathan now bearing down on the car with unstoppable momentum.

'Get out!' Warren groped past Angela and flung open the passenger door, pushing the girl out of the car in the same motion.

Desperately he twisted the ignition key but for once that mighty V8 failed to fire, its giant Holley carburettors flooded by the driver's panic stricken kicks at the throttle.

The starter motor wailed uselessly. Warren leapt

out, bending over the bonnet, straining with every muscle and sinew to push the big coupe off the tracks.

'Warren, leave it!' Angela, half way down the embankment, seemed on the verge of going back to assist. 'You're mad. Leave the bloody car. It's not stopping – the train's not stopping!' She hesitated, for the Monaro appeared to be rolling, ever so slowly, backwards.

Almost imperceptibly, inch by tortuous inch, the vehicle moved, but both it and the driver were already bathed in a milky phosphorescent glare, pouring in a spreading beam from the train's bluff cylindrical snout. Again the girl screamed, for the engine's cowcatcher was now just metres away from Warren and his machine.

For a split second, Angela thought she saw the Holden gathering pace: then all at once the train was overhead, and shrieking past, with the scorching breath of its furnace blasting down like a *sirocco*. And with the sound and heat and smell there flashed a view – a fleeting, dreamlike vision – of the cabin. In the fire glow of that antediluvian engine, figures appeared to be leaping about – frenzied, spectral shapes, with one in particular standing out: inchoate, massive, vaguely human in outline, it crouched grotesquely at the cabin door, poised as if ready to spring.

'Warren!' There had been no crash, no rending of metal. Angela raced up the bank, hopes welling as she crested the metal tracks. Sure enough, there was the Monaro, virtually unscathed, its tail-end halfway through a barbed wire fence, its body at an angle to the tracks and its Mag wheels buried in loose gravel. 'Warren!' Her second shout echoed through an eerie silence.

'Stop mucking around,' the young woman demanded, walking tentatively toward the car. 'Where are you, Warren?'

Through the almost palpable hush that had settled across the moonlit forest and farmland there came no reply. Warren was not in the car. Nor was he in the scrub. The only sign of his passing was a single rubber sandal, dangling at the edge of the track. Angela slumped back against the bonnet of the Monaro, her mind over-wrought and her body exhausted. For long minutes after the passage of that strange train, the silence was absolute. No bird twittered, no dog barked. Until finally a 350 cubic inch Chevrolet engine burst into life and Angela, revving and sliding the car free of its gravel holding bay, drove as fast as she dared to the nearest village, and the welcoming glow of a public telephone.

Chapter Two
Sunday 10th July 1977 – Sydney, New South Wales

'MIRAMBEENA GHOST TRAIN Strikes Again – Top Business Woman Missing'. It seemed a typical tabloid headline, shrieking its message from wire-framed posters outside news stands and convenience stores across the city.

For one Sunday morning observer, however, it held greater significance. Tessa Scott had just finished a weekend session of *pro bono* work in her quayside legal chambers, and noticed the billboard as she left the building. She had lived in the Mirambeena region as a child, and knew the area well. She also knew Jemima Blackman – 31 year old Managing Director of Bishop Industrial Gases, board member of several other blue chip companies, think tank guru and aspiring politician – whose attractive face was captioned by the banner headlines.

Tessa paid for a newspaper and without taking her eyes from the front page, walked toward her car. 'Something murky is going on in Queensland's Mirambeena Valley,' the story opened, 'and the mystery cannot simply be dismissed as the product of fertile imaginations.' Well, the tone of this article was certainly a far cry from those early reports of Warren Schultz's bizarre disappearance, just on a fortnight ago. Where, Tessa wondered, had all the cynicism gone? In the beginning, reporters had openly derided eye-witness Angela Reimann's version of events – the mysterious train rushing down the disused track, the Monaro's close escape, the rubber thong found dangling from the railway sleeper.

The weight of popular opinion had also been against Angela. According to much hotel and office gossip – mostly by people who had never met her – the young woman was simply a jezebel, who had tired of her rev-head boyfriend and devised some sinister yet effective means of permanently ditching him. The idea that someone would resort to such an outlandish and implausible tale in order to conceal a murder had raised surprisingly few doubts within the ranks of Miss Reimann's judges.

But then came the *second* disappearance – this time of a middle-aged potato farmer, who vanished from the same locality a few days after Warren Schultz. When several more witnesses came forward to report train sightings, on other officially-abandoned sections of track, a profound shift in public and media perceptions began to gather momentum. The legend of the 'Mirambeena Ghost Train' was suddenly off and running. To some it was the clanking, hissing reincarnation of the infamous *Diablo*, the great British-designed locomotive which had crashed on its maiden journey to the Darling Downs fifty odd years ago. To others it was, both literally and figuratively, nothing more than one gigantic hoot.

'So! What to do?' Tessa Scott was still reading – and indeed was now talking to herself – as she stepped out onto the footpath, oblivious to any passers-by and their curious sidelong glances. She had once described herself to a work colleague as 'merely a dilettante and a card-carrying nosey parker', but she came from a background where community involvement and acting in the broader public interest were long-standing and cherished traditions. 'Those who are doing well out of society have to put back' – those words, widely attributed to her great-grandfather, had acquired the status of family motto, and though their intention might never have been to send a young, single woman haring off on some sort of unofficial gumshoe exercise, they now had the effect of focussing Tessa's mind on just such a course.

'Well, why not?' It was only last year that she had helped solve a mystery involving hundreds of missing cattle, a case which had baffled official investigators from right across Queensland. What was to stop her taking some more holidays right now, and once again heading north? She could renew some acquaintances perhaps; look up some old haunts? Most of all though, she might be able to make a contribution; lend someone a helping hand.

Amid the welter of nationwide speculation about

a Queensland 'ghost train', Ms Scott had in fact already started some discreet enquiries. Her own firm's librarian, through contacts in various government and media agencies, had checked the frequency of 'missing persons' incidents throughout South East Queensland, concentrating on an area that stretched between the Bremer River and the eastern Darling Downs, northward to Kingaroy and south to Warwick. According to official records and newspaper reports, the recent disappearances of Warren Schultz and farmer Arnie Scheiwe had taken to sixteen the number of people who had vanished in the Mirambeena district over the past twelve months. This figure was far higher than any state or national average, and so far not one of these unfortunate people had been located by police or other agencies. By any measure, it was a bizarre state of affairs.

And what on earth was Jemima Blackman doing up in that neck of the woods? The details in the Sunday newspaper were frustratingly sketchy. Ms Blackman, on a business trip to Brisbane and various regional Queensland centres, had last been seen in the little village of Pilton. She had apparently stayed in a Toowoomba motel on the evening of July 7th but her distinctive red Jaguar XJS had been positively identified in a couple of out of the way spots the following day. It was assumed – by the reporter for this tabloid at least – that she was sightseeing and may have driven up some quiet back-road to enjoy some bushwalking. *Bush-walking*? As generous toward her fellows as Tessa habitually was, she could not suppress a feeling of incredulity at the prospect of Jem Blackman, in hiking boots and parka, climbing through barbed wire fences and clambering up wallaby trails.

'Uh-uh, not she!' Tessa vigorously shook her head. Visions of Jemima did come floating to mind – but they were visions of exquisitely coiffed and lacquered blonde hair, gold-strapped stiletto-heeled shoes and a magnificently patterned sun-frock from a Milanese couturier. Ah! Now that was Jemima. That was exactly how she had looked, in fact, at that university senate meeting back in April, the last time that she and Tessa had seen each other.

And what a meeting that had been: the two newest members of the senate, their youth and gender setting them apart, each something of a novelty in those hallowed halls ... Ms Blackman, frequently on her feet, raising the ire of a number of faculty representatives with her sweeping proposals for across the board salary cuts and a virtual halving of arts faculty funding. Some departments would be closed, several courses in history, medieval literature and music would be abandoned and at least twenty lecturers from the 'non-productive' disciplines – to use Jemima's terminology – would be retrenched.

When asked whether redundancy packages

would be offered, Jemima's tone had been more than usually acid.

'Perhaps you should have been saving up,' she told the department head who had dared to pose the question. 'That's the trouble these days – no concept of self-reliance.'

Thankfully, the proposals had received very little support from other senate members, either then or since, but for one fleeting moment now, Tessa allowed her imagination free rein – just long enough to see a harried Jemima, hair matted and adrift, pursued across a scrub-choked Queensland gully by some wild-eyed, tweed-coated, Chaucer-sprouting denizen of a sandstone university.

'Don't be stupid,' the young lawyer told herself angrily, as a pang of guilt ushered back the reality that Ms Blackman was quite possibly in considerable danger – whoever or whatever the culprit, this was clearly not a joking matter. 'Where on earth could she – ?' Tessa's voice trailed off, for the realisation had also dawned that she was speaking aloud and that several passers-by were not only eyeing her off, but were taking considerable pains to walk well clear of her.

'Whoops!' Face reddening, the girl quickly stepped off the kerb and lowered her tall frame into the cosy confines of a Fiat 124 Sport Coupe, which took off with a snarling exhaust and a chirp from the rear tyres.

A SUNDAY AFTERNOON at home and an evening at a harbourside cocktail party did little to dispel Tessa Scott's nagging thoughts about the fate of Jemima Blackman, Warren Schultz and all the others who had vanished among the farmlands and foothills of the Mirambeena Valley. The reading of some case reports, the writing of a brief opinion and even a martial arts practice session, were all tackled with less than her usual concentration. And later, as she crested the waves of elegantly attired guests at an art gallery soirée, Tessa's mind kept floating back through the sea of small talk; not just to the recent spate of mysterious disappearances, but to a series of childhood and teenage recollections – of school days and bush holidays; of quiet byways and gravel back-roads that wandered among scrub-clad hills. Those visions were scented by the rich fragrance of lantana, and accompanied by the *crack* of whipbirds, ringing amidst the chatter of creeks tumbling over concrete crossings.

But a *train*? A steam locomotive, of all things, years after the last one had seen active service. This was surely a mystery worth solving. One to easily rival last year's investigation into sightings of *Thylacoleo Carnifex*[1], when Tess and a few other

[1] The famed 'Marsupial Lion', whose bite strength reputedly exceeded that of any other carnivore, extant or extinct. Details of this expedition will be released in the future.

amateurs shed new light on the habits of one of Australia's most unusual predators. This train affair was back in the same region – a place where intimate local knowledge just might make a difference.

'OK then!' Tess decided suddenly, and very nearly aloud. The issue could no longer be denied or postponed! It was all very well having professional success: the well-tailored clothes, the city practice, the rewards of a job well done – so much of the city life was enriching, stimulating, and downright fun at times. But for Tess there was also the bush – the opportunity to be a part *of* nature, rather than apart *from* the natural elemental forces – and that was a side of her personality she could never suppress for too long. Her father, the Honourable Leslie Scott M.P., New England grazier, solicitor and businessman, often used to tease her about being 'Clancy's lawyer' – doing well in town but still hankering after the 'better country, further out'. Her brother Andrew claimed that every so often she just needed to head for the scrub and turn maenad.

Les Scott had, in fact, imbued both his children with a wide range of interests. Never favouring the male sibling in any activity, he had taught them both at an early age how to ride, how to shoot, how to fish, but most of all how to love and respect the outdoors, and the ongoing nature of things. Throughout their education, he had shown them rare and exquisite connections between literature, art and the wider environment; had shown them how diversity, tolerance and tradition could meld and weld rather than fracture; had watched their city careers flourish, refreshed and renewed through countryside contact.

For Tess then, it was time once again to escape the confines. A chambers conference in the morning, a few hours work to round off her present brief, and she knew she could be free for a fortnight at least. She packed a suitcase late that Sunday evening and on Monday morning she approached Derek Anstruther, a partner in whom she had enormous trust, to take over any work which might crop up over the next couple of weeks – or, if necessary, until further notice.

'You can repay the favour,' the bouncy, impeccably-suited Anstruther told her as she left the office at just after 2 pm, 'on the last week of the ski season. Just be sure you're back by then, mate.'

'I'll be here, Snow Bunny,' Tessa grinned. A moment later, her Fiat was burbling up out of the underground car-park, darting across the Harbour Bridge and, by missing most of the peak hour traffic, was soon heading up the expressway. From Newcastle, her track was to the North-West, so that late evening found her in the old family homestead on Waverley Downs, in the fastnesses of the New England Ranges.

Leslie Scott, at home for the parliamentary recess, made a light supper for his daughter while listening to her views on the events in Queensland and her plans for an unofficial 'reconnaissance'.

'I've got a bit of work on here at the station just at present, or I could perhaps come with you. Then again, you need to look at these things independently, I suppose. I know you'll be careful.' He was pouring coffee as he spoke, projecting a figure that somehow combined old world grace and homely practicality in virtually equal measure, with all the while a pent-up vigour and alertness that belied his sixty-three years. How many men still wore a cravat these days, Tess wondered – although she could think of one other who still might – and were those steel grey sideburns a touch of current decade fashion or a throwback to the Victorian epoch with which her father always claimed affinity?

'I certainly will be careful, dad. You taught us all that, I reckon.' Tess grinned up at him, stirring her percolated brew well before changing the subject. 'You're not lonely here these days?' The break-up of her parents' marriage had been hard on both parties, but the glare of publicity had surely been worse for her father, a private man in a world becoming increasingly raucous and intrusive.

'Why would I be, dear? I've got a blessed housekeeper, a station manager with a wife and child, and several jackaroos in the living quarters within shouting distance. It's hard to get any peace sometimes. Of course, I didn't want to wake Mrs. Wallace when you arrived – she might have welcomed another cuppa, but she's not long gone to bed. Your mother's new production seems to be going well, if the crowd the other night is any indication. Have you been to see it?'

'I went on opening night.' It was typical of her father's approach to life, Tess reflected, that when her mother had left to restart her truncated career as a playwright and producer, he had not only wished her well but had followed and supported that career avidly, attending all her productions, assisting in whatever ways he could. Conservative he might be – even stubborn occasionally – but Leslie Scott was always a man of positive outlook and few regrets; except perhaps for his perennial annoyance with many on his own side of politics, mostly for their failure to understand and appreciate the relationship between indigenous Australians and the land. But he was working on that issue vigorously as well, particularly now that he was in cabinet, alongside a Prime Minister of like mind and similar priorities.

Chapter Three
7:45am Tuesday 12th July 1977 – Waverley Downs Station, near Armidale, New South Wales

ICE CRACKLED BENEATH Tessa Scott's boots as she strode through the homestead gate to the waiting Fiat coupe. She turned to hug her father.

'I swear you're getting taller,' he joked, looking up slightly into her brown eyes. 'How old are you now?'

'Um, 29, dad. I think I reached my full height just a little while ago.'

'I should jolly well hope so,' Leslie Scott smiled ruefully. 'Oh well, it was always the women who had the height advantage in this family. Your mother's five foot ten in bare feet, the same as you. Your brother and I, meanwhile, must have inherited short, stocky genes.'

'Well, it didn't hold back your Rugby Union careers,' Tess smiled.

'No, perhaps not. Anyway, just to reiterate what we were talking about last night, Tess: do be careful, won't you? And remember, it's generally a bit warmer up in those parts. You'll recall when we had holdings on the Downs and down near Mirambeena – some of the days may be quite warm, and there may be snakes out and about. Long pants are the order of the day. Do you remember that red-bellied black travelling on *top* of the long grass, down along Whipbird Creek?'

'I certainly do. As clearly as if it happened yesterday.'

'Will you call in and check over that Junction Ridge bush block that we sold to Johnno while you're up there? He's always inviting us to stay in the old hut, away from any mod-cons. It's a great spot to catch up on some "r & r", if you get time.'

'It certainly sounds tempting,' Tess sighed. 'I'll just have to see how things work out with this little line of enquiry, I suppose. Well dad, I hate to run but I reckon I should try to put some distance behind me.'

The 1600cc, twin overhead camshaft engine burst into life and with a cheery toot of the air horns, Tessa trundled off down the track toward Waverley's front gates, picking her way carefully around potholes out of respect for the car's low ground clearance. Once out on bitumen road she let the little machine have its head, the rising and falling engine note combining with the burbling exhaust to send a minor symphony echoing through the granite outcrops and wafting across the ridges on the still morning air. It seemed almost as if the petite Italian coupe had caught the mood of adventure and anticipation enjoyed by its driver, as if it too was keen and alert to the possibilities, while they darted north along the New England Highway.

Though she scanned the road carefully before and behind, and appreciated the scenery as much as practicable, Tessa was now thoroughly focussed on her destination, the mystery, and a strategy for the days ahead. Unofficial this investigation might be, but she was nonetheless determined to get results, to crack this conundrum if she possibly could. She mulled once more over lines of enquiry, and of possible cover. There were take-apart fishing rods on the back seat, while in the boot her Browning 2 shot auto, the 'double automatic', sat in its zippered bag beside her suitcase. It was the duck and quail season and she had already applied for a license. There were properties in the vicinity of the last three disappearances that she was welcome to visit for hunting or fishing.

The young woman thought too of the telegram she had sent from Sydney the previous morning, and the follow-up phone call she had made last night from Waverley. The recipient of those messages also knew something of the Mirambeena region, and like her he could seldom resist a mystery.

9am, Monday 11th July 1977. Oxford University, England.

'GOOD MORNING, PROFESSOR. This telegram actually came through last night. I thought you might like to read it first thing, before you started work as such.'

'Good morning, Rosemary – and thank you.' Professor Hugh Bainbridge, of Oxford University's English Language and Literature faculty, accepted his bundle of mail and unfolded the telegram which the secretary had placed carefully atop the pile. Putting on his spectacles in a calm, almost languid manner, he read :

> DEAREST HUGH stop HAVE MYSTERY TO RIVAL LAST YEAR'S stop SAME DISTRICT stop IF NOT TOO BUSY COME OUT stop IF BUSY COME ANYWAY stop EN ROUTE TODAY WILL PHONE TONIGHT stop LOVE TESS.

'Bossy Boots!' The professor smiled broadly. 'So, another mystery, eh? Well, we'll see what Miss Muffet has to say when she telephones later.'

Bainbridge now turned his attention to the unsteady tower of books and journals on his office desk, and soon his fountain pen was screeching across the pages of an exercise book – making notes, fashioning paragraphs of argument, jotting down references. A teacher of English literature from 1540 to the present day, Bainbridge included among his wide research interests the study of colonial poetry and prose: in fact, he was presently taking a term off to research and co-write a text book on the latter subject. It seemed somehow appropriate therefore that he was skimming through Clement Semmler's erudite biography of the Australian bush poet A.B. 'Banjo' Paterson, when his phone rang and an Australian of Caledonian heritage came on the line.

'Hugh, you got my telegram?'

'Muffet.' The professor leaned back in his chair, tea cup in one hand and telephone in the other. 'It must be rather a late hour over there. Now what's all this about a mystery? Not mega-fauna again, surely?'

'No, not mega-fauna,' Tess replied. 'But a very large and frightening monstrosity nonetheless. And it appears to be gobbling people up.'

'Animal, vegetable, or mineral?'

'Probably mineral; however, according to some observers, it may not even be material, of any kind. More a spirit of something past.'

'Hmm! Much as I abhor sceptics, anti-romantics, and all that ilk, I fear I simply must play "devil's advocate". Now just what form does this mystical apparition take?'

'Well, it seems to be some sort of ghost train – yes, I know: it does sound weird, but the undeniable fact is that people have been disappearing, leaving no trace. And the same goes for the train itself: after showing up on long disused tracks, it abruptly vanishes into thin air.'

'Actually, I should apologise for being a little distracted,' said Hugh. 'Now that I think of it, I believe your phantom locomotive might have made the tabloid press here just recently.'

'I'm not sure which is the more surprising, Hugh,' Tess laughed. 'The fact that the story made the overseas papers, or the thought of you reading a tabloid.'

'The latter is hard to imagine, I know, but one does such things occasionally, in the absence of jam labels or other more interesting reading matter. So, Tess: the gist of all this is that you want me to travel some 12,000 miles, in pursuit of a train which may, or may not, exist?'

'I'm afraid that's pretty much it. You will come, won't you?'

'Oh well, what better reason?' Professor Bainbridge smiled. 'And I suppose I could always tie in a spot of research on your bush bards – Paterson, Lawson, Boake and all those chaps – to justify my professional existence.'

'So when should I expect you?'

'Hmm. Just bear with me a jiffy while I consider the logistics. I believe British Airways flies daily to Sydney these days. I'll have to organise just a few things at this end before taking off, mainly to do with Booker. He'll require board and lodging. My passport is up to date, so all going to plan, one should arrive in Brisbane around Friday or Saturday.'

'How is old Booker, the darling?'

'Oh, he's the one fixed point in a thoroughly muddled universe; still the epitome of spaniels. He loves activity, so he'll no doubt enjoy a holiday in the countryside for a week or three. And Westmead will love having him.'

'Well thank you, Hugh. I hope this is not putting you out too much, and that it doesn't all turn out to be a wild goose chase. Anyway, I'll be staying at the Bluegum Motel, in Mirambeena, from tomorrow night. You can contact me there if you need to.'

'Excellent. I'll say cheerio then, Muffet, till later in the week.'

As Professor Bainbridge hung up the telephone, the casual observer might have noted a subtle yet profound change in his demeanour. Energy had replaced languor, and though the atmosphere of calm and equanimity remained, there was now vigour and a hint of excitement in the grey blue eyes. With the air of a big cat uncoiled from a noonday nap, he whisked several books and papers into a briefcase, closed the door to his office and strode purposefully down the corridor to a room filled with secretarial desks. Rosemary, the young woman who had earlier delivered his mail and telegram, showed no hint of surprise.

'Should I hold all mail, sir, or forward it on?'

'Hold thank you, Rosemary. I expect to be away at least a month, but if it looks like being much longer than that, I'll be in touch to provide a forwarding address.'

'Certainly Professor. Anything else?'

'Oh, if anyone telephones or leaves any messages to do with colonial poetry, could you direct them to my esteemed co-author, care of the University of New South Wales? I should be in contact with her at least a couple of times while I'm in Australia.'

'Right you are. I'll forward anything of that nature on. Enjoy your trip then, Professor.'

'I shall certainly do my best. Oh, and I *will* send you all a postcard.'

Smiles beamed up from the faculty secretaries' desks, acknowledging the professor's cheery wave and boyish grin before the view changed to a rapidly-departing, tweed coated back. With his air of affability and unfailing politeness, Bainbridge was a popular figure right across the campus, amongst students, professorial colleagues and a wide range of general staff.

Even among the modernists and Marxists in his own discipline, there were many who warmed to his quaint brand of old-world eccentricity, his studied refusal to acknowledge the *zeitgeist.* There were also these sporadic episodes when he seemed to revert to the guards officer of his youth; to transmogrify, in true Renaissance style, into the man of action. Several tutors chuckled knowingly when they saw him striding now through the faculty car park, swinging up and over the door of a Morgan Plus eight, and dropping lithely into the driver's seat. Within minutes, they knew, the professor would be powering the 3.5 litre classic-bodied sports car away from the precincts of town and gown, and off down hedge-lined country lanes – and it would be some time before he returned.

Of course, these traits could also astound and possibly dismay some recent acquaintances, earning Bainbridge nicknames such as 'Zorro' or 'the elusive pimpernel', but had Tess been able to see him at this juncture, she would not have been in the least surprised. She had decided a long time ago that John Buchan's description of Basil Blackwood applied equally to Hugh: *In a pedestrian world he held to the old cavalier grace, and wherever romance called he followed with careless gallantry.*

11.15am, Tuesday 12th July. Ballandean, Queensland.

IN A REST AREA just off the New England Highway, Tessa Scott was sitting atop a rustic wooden picnic table, enjoying the bracing air of the Granite Belt. She had just finished an apricot tart from a nearby bakery and was sipping tea from a vacuum flask while she browsed a local newspaper. Any thoughts that the trail might go cold as she neared it were quickly and firmly dispelled by the journal's page two story.

'DOWNS TEACHER MISSING:' the headline shouted. 'ANOTHER MYSTERY TRAIN SIGHTING.'

Beneath a photo of an earnest looking young man, a captioning paragraph read: '32 year old Toowoomba music teacher Wesley Smythe, last seen in the vicinity of Whipbird Creek, near Mirambeena, on Sunday morning. Locals have reported hearing the sounds of a train, though the nearest stretch of railway was closed over 25 years ago.'

'Whipbird Creek?' Tess taxed her memory of the Mirambeena district, trying to pinpoint the exact location of this latest disappearance relative to earlier incidents. 'Hmm. That's a fair distance, though not too far in a straight line, I suppose. Trouble is, no railway line – not functioning anyway.'

The lawyer read on:

'Wesley Smythe told friends on Sunday morning that he was going for a drive down the range, where he might do some 'hiking, fishing or just exploring'. The alarm was raised when he failed to return to his shared accommodation in Toowoomba on Sunday night, and on Monday morning his Ford Falcon sedan was found, abandoned, not far from a disused railway loop-line near Whipbird Creek. Alf Waters, the local grazier who discovered the car, told this reporter that while having dinner on Sunday evening he had seen a strange light – "for all the world like a train headlight" – but he had quickly dismissed the idea because the loop-line close to his property has not seen service for a quarter of a century and the light did not appear to be following the tracks anyway.'

'So – the mystery deepens.' Tess folded the newspaper, collected her vacuum flask and other belongings and jumped into her car. The best course now was surely to get to the actual locality, as quickly as possible, and look for primary evidence rather than second-hand reports. She made one quick stop for petrol, on the outskirts of the stately old city of Warwick, then sweeping past the big multi-lane intersection which funnelled traffic off to Brisbane via Cunningham's Gap, she took the road to Toowoomba. Well before reaching that bustling city, however, she turned right down a narrow lane which meandered across soft rolling farmland, then plunged down off the Darling Downs in a series of serpentine curves, switchbacks and wooden bridges. For mile after twisting mile, the road then wound its way around the scrub-clad banks of a sinuous mountain creek, where birdsong blended with the snarl of the Fiat's exhaust, and the little car responded to skilful touches of throttle and brake as if it were an extension of the driver. On and on they darted – around towering moss-covered boulders, through fern-laden gullies, past mysterious fissures, crannies and caves – until at last they rushed out into the early afternoon light, and the road widened and straightened out, arrowing on through picturesque open farm-scapes that ran back towards gentle hills. And suddenly there he was – a figure who might have been lifted, with his entire surroundings, from an E.H. Shephard book illustration.

Just like that Artist of the Roman Road in Kenneth Grahame's *Golden Age*, he was seated at work by the roadside. Unlike so many of today's painters, who sat in studios and worked from photographs or sketches, this gentleman was out in the elements, at one with, and part of, his landscape. With palette, easel and folding chair, he seemed somehow fused with his subject, capturing it while it captured him.

There were, of course, certain differences. Unlike Grahame's artist, he did not wear knickerbockers – though to Tessa's mind, his hand-knitted vest and hounds-tooth check trousers seemed to make a pretty reasonable substitute for a homespun suit. Nor did he go afoot, for a Triumph 2000 saloon could be seen reposing cooly in the shade of a nearby fig tree. And against that car door leaned a second painting – not for sale it seemed, for it was not displayed full on to the passing traffic, but Tessa's eye was nonetheless arrested by it.

'Cattle Mountain! But it can't be.' The girl braked, down-shifted and made a cautious U-turn to park behind the Triumph. She knew well that peak, with its grass-tree studded pinnacle rearing up from the saddle-back formation known as Junction Ridge, but there was something different – something that blatantly didn't belong – in this picture. It was a train – a steam train surely – with its unmistakeable trail of smoke billowing up through the trees and lantana scrub as it puffed its way around the lower slopes of the range. Artistic licence? An overwrought imagination? Or had the man sitting nearby, landscape artist in all his being, really seen it?

Harking back to Grahame's warnings about the *genus irritable*, Tessa got out of her car with some trepidation. She approached slowly, a trifle unsure how to broach the subject.

'Hello! Lovely afternoon for it,' the artist beamed. 'I'll be with you in a tick. Just one thing I need to get right, before I down brushes.' Clearly this was an affable soul, though deep in concentration and full of commitment to his task. 'Pull up a rock, why don't you? I'd offer you a chair, but I more or less need this one at present.'

'Good afternoon – oh, and please accept my apologies for the intrusion,' Tess smiled in return. 'There's nothing worse when you're right in the middle of something and you need to focus on it.'

'Not at all. I was about to take a break shortly anyway. Just a touch more azure there, I think. There! "How's that?" as our flannelled fools say.'

'It looks exquisite to me,' Tess said. 'The light and space. And the way the eye travels to the hills and then up. I love the hawk – was he here earlier?'

'Yes – a few hours ago he was hovering over the ploughed paddock there. I seldom invent. I think he missed his mouse, or lizard, or whatever he was after, and headed for different pastures – but I thought I'd leave him in anyway. He adds to the dimension of sky and space, or so I like to think. Would you care for a cuppa? It's only coffee from a vacuum flask, but I might have a spare cup.'

'Thank you.' Tessa nodded toward the cars. 'As long as I'm not cutting you short for later.'

'Not at all. I'll probably only do another half hour or so and then pack it in. The pub where I'm staying at Tent Creek will be able to provide liquid refreshment, I'm sure, without my resorting to more coffee. Oh, my name's Frank Richards by the way, all the way from Brisbane, and you are …?' The artist held out a multi-coloured hand.

'Tessa Scott. And I'm from even further afield – Sydney, believe it or not. I did some of my growing up around here though, and I come up here quite often.'

'Pleased to meet you, Tessa. You know the district well, then?' Frank Richards handed the girl a steaming pannikin and relaxed back on a nearby log. A man of about 40 years of age, he had a friendly, outgoing face which seemed like a perfect window to his personality, though his blue-grey eyes held a faint air of distraction, as if roving constantly toward distant horizons.

'Fairly well, I guess.' Tess glanced toward the Triumph. 'Actually, Frank, there was something I was wondering – about your other painting over there.'

'Oh yes; Cattle Mountain. You know the place? It's not all that far from here.'

'Yes, I recognised it straight off as I drove past. But what threw me a little was the train. I climbed the mountain as a teenager, and as far as I was aware, there were never any railroad tracks within 30 kilometres of that peak. No rail connections of any kind.'

'There were that day,' Frank Richards suggested as they walked over to the painting. 'I must admit though, that I was surprised too. I couldn't locate any railway symbols on the maps I used. And I couldn't actually see any tracks from my vantage point, which was back on a lower rise, a bit to the west. From the course the train took, the tracks must wind right across the base of the ridge that Cattle Mountain rears up from.' The artist pointed at the bottom of his picture. 'The metals must be hidden by this scrub that you see down here in the foreground.'

'Hmm.' Tessa looked thoughtful. 'And yet, Frank, I've explored those scrubby gullies. That's awfully rugged terrain to cut and lay a track through. I wasn't aware that Premier Joh was into any rapid rail building projects, and why so deep in the foothills of the ranges? Some sort of mineral extraction project perhaps? There again, I was up here late last year and I saw and heard nothing about any developments of that type.'

'Neither have I, come to think of it. I ran out of daylight the day I was working over there on this painting – basically I just wanted to finish the picture and get back to the hotel that night, so I didn't go exploring much. But I heard the train, and saw it, I do assure you – even though I was half a mile off.'

'If you don't mind my asking, Frank, how long ago did you paint the picture?'

'Let me see now – today is Tuesday – Saturday, it would have been. I've been just moseying around the district for a couple of days since, looking for a prospect that appealed – until today, when I found this place.'

'Well thank you so much, Frank, for your time – and the cuppa. I'd better let you get back to your work, while there's still plenty of light.'

'It's been a pleasure, Tessa. But yes, you're right – it's amazing how soon the light starts to fade on a July day. And I *do* appreciate light.'

'Well you certainly make wonderful use of it. It's been a privilege to look at your work. Cheers, Frank.'

'Cheerio then.' The artist was strolling back to his current work. 'Enjoy your visit back to the old

Sunshine State, Tessa. Might see you about perhaps.'

'Bye, and thanks again.' Once more Tessa turned the Fiat's nose toward Mirambeena, but a couple of kilometres down the road, at the approaches to a quaint little village, she took a side road to the right, following the signs to Junction Ridge. A half-hour later, her little car was parked just off the road below Cattle Mountain and the young lawyer was carefully negotiating the unforgiving strands of a tautly-strung barbed wire fence.

Once she was in the paddock, Tessa padded off along tracks filled with memories, plunging between pungent clumps of lantana, following wallaby and cattle pads up lightly-forested spurs, past the myriad scrub-choked gullies etched into the western slopes of Cattle Mountain, and the long ridge which it topped.

Ah, what recollections! That tangle of boulders up near the ridge crest, hiding a secret rocky gorge; those magical, deep-cut ravines scoring the hillside, their vine and tree clad upper slopes concealing sheer cliffs of multi-coloured stone. For the best part of three hours, Tessa searched the escarpment, until the gathering dusk found her back at the little coupe, drinking gratefully the last remnants of tea from her vacuum flask.

'Frank was wrong. He must have been.' Tessa spoke the words aloud, as a sudden shudder, unrelated either to the chill of the approaching night or the far-off howl of a dingo, niggled at her shoulder blades. One thing was now certain, and Tessa's searches of the afternoon had proved it beyond reasonable doubt – if the artist *had* seen a train in this vicinity, it was one which had no need of rail-road tracks.

Chapter Four

'Ah, the *Diablo* – that old devil train!'

P*ICTURE IF YOU WILL a scene of pure impressionism, a vibrant tableau where many details stand out stark and clear but a million mysteries might still lie hidden beneath the broad, thick layers of the brush. A shouting man points to the crest of a verdant hill, where a glistening monster, its coal-black flanks streaked with fiery red, slides to a halt. It snorts expectantly, as if sniffing the wind, pulsing with raw energy before it swoops into the grassy dales below.*

A triumphant bellow! – and the gleaming locomotive charges forward and down, thundering across the rolling diorama, blasting past creeks and cultivated fields, darting through small villages and level crossings to the strident accompaniment of bells and whistles: then hammering into a long dank tunnel and out over a high arched bridge spanning a rock-strewn gorge.

It slows now, just perceptibly, to negotiate a long sweeping curve, and then it's full steam ahead for another short furious straight across a picturesque farm-scape. Two watchers stand motionless, transfixed by the unfolding drama, as the steam engine, like a runaway car of Juggernaut, hauls its tender, van and trio of carriages toward a steeply-banked bend, with a curved bridge and a terrifying, yawning abyss, just visible beyond.

Too late, a scream of brakes! The great train twists and coils, bucking wildly and crumpling like a concertina as it flies clear of the metals and floats into the chasm beyond the track. And then two giant hands, cupped together, clutch swiftly at the locomotive and carriages, rescuing the exquisite models mere inches from the mosaic tiled floor….

'My apologies for the anti-climax, Professor.' With his little show over, the speaker was now carefully reinstating his toys upon a huge table, the centrepiece of a room which housed the most spectacular and detailed model railway systems his guest had ever seen. 'I'd hate to write off something as beautifully crafted as this model of the *Diablo*, just for the sake of adding authenticity to a demonstration.'

'Indeed.' Hugh Bainbridge accepted a glass of sherry from his host and sipped appreciatively. 'And you've no need to apologise, I assure you. I must say, Mr Wyatt, that was a remarkable demonstration, right down to the last detail. You certainly have an incredible collection – and such a variety of landscapes and track configurations to trial them in.'

'Playthings, Professor, when all is said and done.' James Wyatt, a stocky, rubicund man with a vast shock of unruly grey hair, waved his glass dismissively. 'Mere playthings. Not quite like the real McCoy, you know – the smell of coal fire, the hiss of steam. I designed and built 'em, of course, when it was the only way to travel. In fact, I was on the design team for this very locomotive – the famous, or possibly infamous, *Diablo*. But I imagine that's what put you on to me, the reason you're here. You would have gleaned that sort of background information from that confounded tabloid newspaper report, about the Australian business. I expect the article rabbited on about the *Diablo* and linked me to its construction, particularly as I'm the last surviving member of the original design team.'

'Yes, that article did more or less lead me to your door, Mr Wyatt. Or at any rate, it gave me the idea to phone you. And it was very kind of you to see me, especially at such short notice. You see, I'm actually heading off to Australia in a day or so. A friend of mine down there is investigating this spate of disappearances associated with the train, and I thought before I left it might be an idea to obtain a bit of authoritative background information on the machine itself.'

'I can certainly give you that.' The older man's face flushed an even more fiery red. 'I was involved in the *Diablo* project from start to finish – design, manufacture, export. What I didn't agree with was the use of such a powerful engine design on such a narrow frame – they run only a three foot six gauge in the state of Queensland, you know – and I believe that made the *Diablo* inherently unstable at its maximum.'

'You'll forgive my ignorance I'm sure, Mr Wyatt, for I'm no engineer. But I was just wondering about the diesel and electric trains in use on narrow gauge tracks today. Would they not have even higher speed potential?'

'Ah yes; but suspension and frame design have now advanced enormously. Nowadays they employ all sorts of technologies to enhance stability – things which were never even on the drawing board back in my day. Tilt is the coming thing, let me tell you, and tilt technology will allow high speed trains to travel as safely on narrow gauge as they do on standard or broad gauge.'

'I see. Well, Mr Wyatt, you've convincingly demonstrated some of the shortcomings of the original *Diablo*, and how it met its end. I wonder now – what do you make of this present business in the Antipodes? Do you think it possible that someone might have reconstructed the *Diablo* – or perhaps made a fully functioning replica – and is prowling about with it? Though the mind boggles as to any conceivable motive.'

'Well, it wouldn't be an easy thing to build in secret, or to move around.' The engineer knitted his brows thoughtfully. 'I gather from certain reports that it's turning up on various disused and disconnected tracks, so how does one account for that? Perhaps a lorry, with a low loader, drive off/drive on at either end? Mind you, it would have to be quite some lorry, towing an absolutely massive trailer, to haul a hundred and fifty tons of locomotive, plus carriages.'

'Indeed. And to what purpose? Could it be the work of some diehard bunch of steam enthusiasts, out to make a statement?'

'Surely not.' James Wyatt shook his head. 'Oh, mind you, there are a few isolated squads of radical steam loyalists in this country, including a few who've gone as far as staging protests and demonstrations over the years since steam was phased out. But they're hardly the types to resort to kidnapping – or worse! I mean, according to these newspaper reports, people have simply vanished, without trace, in the vicinity of this Queensland train, and there seems to be outright criminality involved. Unless, of course, it's all a gigantic hoax or publicity stunt.'

'Hmm, the whole thing quite beggars the imagination.' Hugh was keen to range amongst the possibilities, using his host's clearly vast expertise and experience. 'Are you aware of any organisations in Australia dedicated to maintaining or rebuilding steam engines, Mr Wyatt?'

'Well, now that you mention it, I did receive a letter – at least a year ago it was – from this chap in Ipswich; Ipswich, South East Queensland that is, not ours here in the UK. The writer was some sort of investment consultant, though an engineer by training, and he was urging me to join some world-wide organisation dedicated to the preservation of steam. As I recall, he was particularly keen to promote steam as a modern and viable form of propulsion and to push for its eventual re-introduction on the world's major train routes.'

'Hmm. Sounds like an interesting chap.'

'Wouldn't he be close to the area that you'll be visiting, professor? Perhaps you could look him up? I have his address right here.' Wyatt extracted a letter from a bulging sheaf in a nearby filing cabinet and handed it to Bainbridge. 'Now there's a name for a steam man,' the old engineer whistled as he pointed to the letterhead. 'Maurice J. Arblaster, Investment Consultant, Limestone Street, Ipswich. What a handle, eh? Well, good luck to him. I'm no real friend of internal combustion, I must say – everyone racing about in motors, choking up the roads, taking the romance out of travel. And the diesel train – well, it doesn't have half the glamour of steam, you'd have to admit.'

'No argument from me there,' Hugh chuckled. 'Do you think he might be onto something – with this resurgence of steam idea?'

The engineer shook his head sagely. 'How old are you, professor, if you don't mind my asking?'

'Forty-five.'

'Ah, a mere youth. I've got nearly thirty years on you. I was a qualified engineer at the age of twenty-two and, if I do say so myself, quite a talented steam engine designer at the age of twenty-three. An 'up and coming' they called me then – a 'young man in a hurry'. Of course, my youth meant that not too many of my ideas were actually taken seriously. I've already hinted at the way I was over-ruled in the *Diablo* project, and if ever a piece of machinery needed further development before it was turned loose, it was that monster. Anyway, be that as it may, I could see that the writing was on the wall for steam even back then. Diesel was the coming thing, and since then of course, electricity. Who knows what in future – linear induction, jet propulsion, nuclear, solar. Who knows?'

'Well, thank you again for granting me an interview at such short notice, Mr Wyatt, and for that demonstration of the *Diablo*'s – er – demise. I travel south much better informed.'

'Take care then, Professor Bainbridge. Enjoy your flight, sir, and oh – do be careful of ghost trains, won't you?' James Wyatt chortled as he escorted his guest out on to the porch of his country villa. It was a perfect July afternoon, and Booker the Springer Spaniel gave hearty voice to it from the passenger seat of Bainbridge's Morgan as they trundled off down the elm-bordered driveway. The dog's excited barks, the chatter of birds in the hedgerows, the bleat of sheep in the neighbouring fields, even the growl of the car's compact V8, were all fitting accompaniment to the day's bucolic splendour.

'*In a somer seson when softe was the sonne*,' the Professor murmured, soul and sub-conscious mind transported, for a fleeting moment, into some remote corner of Langland's England that had refused to acknowledge the centuries. Indeed, at that instant, on such a golden afternoon, the idea of fiery trains going 'clank' in the night seemed not just 600 years but a million miles away. And yet reality was still there, niggling and nudging him towards action: a friend had called, a challenge was beckoning and, when all was said and done, a Queensland winter was hardly an uninviting prospect. Hugh swung the Morgan southward, back onto a major road, and half an hour's brisk motoring found him turning up the drive to another country estate.

'Welcome back, sir.' The speaker was a tanned, well-groomed and vigorous looking man of perhaps sixty, who had appeared unobtrusively beside the Morgan almost before the wire-spoked wheels had come to rest. Known to friends – and a few enemies – simply as Westmead, he had been batman to Hugh's father and was now a sort of butler come household manager on the Bainbridge family holdings.

'Hello, Westmead. Good to see you, old chap.' Hugh shook the man's hand warmly as he alighted from the car.

'I've laid out some kit on the bed for you, sir. I know you said on the telephone that you'd be doing some stalking, but as it's in the Antipodes I didn't imagine you'd be wanting full highland gear. I've included a couple of jackets, for I know it's winter down under, but not the heavier tweeds. Oh, and hats, sir: the pith helmet or the Akubra?'

'Hmm. Both perhaps. No, we'd better make it the ratting cap and the Akubra – the helmet seems to amuse certain parties down there.'

'As you say, sir. Oh, and I've taken the liberty of parcelling up the Rigby, and arranging the necessary customs clearance.'

'Thank you, Westmead. You've anticipated everything, as usual.'

'And Booker – the usual exercise and diet, sir?'

'Yes please. Take out the Cashmore, if you like. Oh, will you join me for a drink before dinner? There are a couple of matters where I could use your advice, particularly on a couple of those tumbling manoeuvres and ju-jitsu strikes – I'm having trouble perfecting those.'

'A pleasure, sir.' The retainer then nodded sagely. 'You're suspecting foul play with this train business, aren't you, master Hugh?'

'There has to be some rational explanation, Westmead, and I venture to hope that I'll have a better appreciation of the business in a few days time. But first, there's an abysmal 30-hour plane trip to contend with – ugh!'

'If one might make so bold, sir, there's always a good book.'

Chapter Five
2.45pm Thursday 14th July. Mirambeena, Queensland.

THE OWNER OF Mirambeena's single coffee shop seemed rather nervous, if extremely anxious to please. He also had to admit to feeling a trifle inquisitive, as he showed two attractive first time customers to a cosy alcove, drew out their chairs and handed each a menu.

What could they have in common – this tall, elegant, almost exotic-looking girl in black slacks and long sleeve shirt, with silky, dark brown hair falling on her shoulders, and the petite younger one in the mini-skirt, with corn-coloured locks cut in a fashionable wedge-shaped bob. He was pretty sure he had seen the blonde around town before, though never in his coffee shop, but the other – well, she was a downright mystery, and their opening snippets of conversation were enough to further stimulate a fellow's natural curiosity.

'I appreciate your talking to me, Angela,' Tessa Scott remarked as they sat down. 'Especially as I'm not conducting what you could call an official investigation. It's really good of you to take the time.'

'Oh well,' Angela Reimann shrugged and lit a cigarette. 'The way I see it, I've talked to just about everyone else – police, newspapers, you name it.

When you rang, I thought – oh, bugger it, I might as well talk to you too.'

'Well, thank you again. What will you have? My treat.'

'Thanks. I haven't had an apricot Danish in ages. And a cappuccino sounds good. Actually, I'm really hungry – didn't get much time for lunch.'

'Mmm. Me too.' Tessa attracted the owner's attention and ordered the same for herself and Angela.

'So you're a lawyer, you were saying,' Angela regarded Tessa steadily. 'Are you representing someone connected with this train business?'

'No, I'm not actually representing anyone at the moment.' Tess met the younger woman's enquiring gaze, impressed by her intelligence, forthrightness and the amazingly amiable stoicism she displayed, particularly after what she had been through over the past week or two. 'I do know one of the missing people, however, and because I used to be familiar with the area – well, I thought I'd just take some holidays and try to find something out.'

'Now I'm guessing the one you know is the Sydney businesswoman – Jemima, er, Blackman, is it?' A slight grin flickered for an instant on Angela's face as she considered her next sentence. 'Sorry, I know I can be a bit blunt sometimes. It's just that, well, from the write-ups in the papers and the TV reports, you look like you'd have a lot in common. You seem – well – a bit alike somehow. Is she a close friend, then?'

'Hmm – more of an acquaintance I suppose.' Tess smiled reassuringly, though she had to secretly admit that she did not altogether enjoy the comparison. No doubt Jemima had her good points – her disarming affability, wit and charm were legendary – but her trademark gilt-edged abrasiveness was a trifle hard to take at times. 'We went to university together, and we still have connections there. I certainly would like to try to find her, and Warren and all the others too.'

At the mention of Warren's name, Angela's expression seemed to harden a little. 'Yeah, well, of course, according to a lot of people out there, I'm supposed to have done my boyfriend in. I'm sorry Tessa – I s'pose I have got a few chips on my shoulder about this whole business. It's just that – well, poor bloody Warren goes missing, and I actually saw the train, no further than from here to the back of the coffee shop away! I swore all that in a statement to the police, but does anyone believe me – no! Even some of the newspaper reports seemed to hint that I was making it all up. But, of course, when a big interstate businesswoman goes missing, then it's all different. Then the reports of ghost trains and phantom expresses and secret kidnap plots come out of the woodwork.'

'Yes, the rumour mill can be very, very unfair,' Tess said softly. 'I've seen it in action many a time, with clients who for some reason don't happen to catch the public's imagination or sympathy.'

'Oh well, I'll get over it.' Angela sipped her recently-arrived cappuccino and nibbled the accompanying Danish. 'Do you believe there's a train, Tessa?'

'Yes. You obviously saw it, and so have other people – and in places where a train simply has no right being. The question we have to address is why? Why are people, from all walks of life, being grabbed? Certainly it's not hard to imagine the head of a multi-million dollar corporation becoming a kidnapping target – although if extortion is the game, it's surprising that no ransom demands have been made as yet.'

'Yeah, and why would anyone want to kidnap ordinary working people? No one in their right mind would think Warren had any big money, or connections.' Angela suddenly radiated another of her disarming smiles, which surprisingly never seemed too far away. 'Although, come to think of it, a few of his mates reckon they'd do just about anything to get hold of his Monaro.'

Both women laughed – the sort of tension-relieving laughter that helps participants in any serious situation to cope and explore pathways forward.

They then turned their attention in earnest to their food and beverages, so that it was a minute or two before conversation resumed.

'Did you happen to see anyone in the train, Angela?' Tessa eventually enquired. 'Any passengers in the carriages, or a driver in the locomotive?'

'Well, I remember that there were only a couple of carriages. And in one of them at least, there was a faint glow of lighting. As for the engine, well, you're probably going to think this is weird if I tell you.'

'Try me,' Tess smiled reassuringly.

'Well, I've been thinking back on this, ever since the night it happened; and I'm sure, almost positive in fact, that I did see someone in the cab. There might have been two people – they were only shapes or outlines that I took in really, because I just sort of glanced up quickly and then looked back for Warren. But I could almost swear there were figures leaping about in the fire-glow and that there was one huge man, getting ready to jump.'

'Really? Getting ready to jump?' Tess looked puzzled. 'Can you describe his actions?'

'Well, he was sort of leaning forward, bending towards the doorway.'

'You told this to the police?' At first blush, the scene just described seemed like the product of a frenzied, over-wrought imagination, yet the speaker was so down to earth and genuine that

Tessa found herself accepting it at face value. 'Could they provide any plausible explanation?'

'The police! Yeah well, they've been a bit of a disappointment really. Oh, the first one I spoke to was OK – he was a young local constable – but then the CIB blokes came in from outa town and took over the whole investigation. Bloody hell, did they give me the third degree? For a while I thought they were gonna charge me with something and I talked to me dad about actually getting a lawyer. Anyway, nothing came of that – although I'm sure one of 'em is still following me – it's like he's keeping tabs on me.'

'Really? A plain clothes policeman?'

'Yeah. An Inspector Jensen, or something like that, he was called. He was hanging around just outside the store where I work this morning, and I saw him again out on the footpath, not long before I came here to meet you.'

'That is very unusual procedure, Angela.' Tessa shook her head in amazement. 'If he keeps it up, and you feel harassed by it, I'd be quite happy to have a talk with him and ask him what it's all about. No fees. Here, I'll give you my card – the phone number of the motel where I'm staying is written on the back.'

'Thanks Tessa. I must admit I thought it was a bit strange. I always thought they had to more or less charge you with something or leave you alone, not bloody-well stalk around after you. I mean to say, I don't mind answering questions; I wouldn't even mind if they did do a bit of occasional surveillance – I could understand that, but it feels a bit weird to see a detective every time you turn around.'

'It *is* weird. Ah, here's our host.' Tessa smiled up at the coffee shop owner as he jovially approached their tables.

'How's it going, ladies?' the man enquired. 'Anything else I can get for you now?'

'Not for me, thank you,' Tess replied. 'That was delicious. How about you, Angela?'

'I'm fine thanks, although that was more-ish. Better watch the waistline, though.' As the man took away their crockery, Angela turned back towards the lawyer. 'I really should be getting back to work, Tessa, but if you think I can be of any more help with your investigation, I'd be happy to help. Oh, most of my friends call me Angie or just Ange, too.'

'Thanks, Angie. Oh, I have a friend – a man called Hugh Bainbridge – arriving from England tomorrow. He'd like to help out as well. He has a very analytical sort of mind and often sees things from a slightly different angle. On Saturday, I was thinking of taking him out to the crossing where you saw the train. I was just wondering if you might feel up to joining us out there? Perhaps it might help to jog the old memory – you know, recall a few things that might provide clues – and you could bring both Hugh and I up to speed on the area around there?'

'Yep. No worries,' Angela Reimann replied. 'If I can do anything – anything at all that might help to find Warren, or those other people, just give me a buzz.' She paused for a moment, shaking her head. 'It's amazing, eh? Even people from England getting interested now – I mean, like your friend coming all the way out here.'

'Well, it's a professional trip too – research to do with his job.' Tessa felt a sudden urge to explain. 'But he'll be very happy to lend a hand. He loves a challenge.'

Angie's little smile suggested she was making some 'are they; aren't they' guesses. Tessa smiled in return: it was so much easier to skirt around these things, and simply let people speculate. It had been her preferred strategy since she was a postgraduate student at Oxford, where she had been introduced to Hugh after one of his public lectures. The rumours had started the first time they were seen together around campus, the chatter increasing in pitch and volume whenever they were observed in restaurants or out on picnics with the professor's Springer Spaniel. Well, the gossip and speculation would have to continue for a while yet. Separated for long spells by careers and continents, Tessa and Hugh were content, in the words of the old song, to 'let the rest of the world go by'.

Chapter Six
3.15pm Friday 15th July – Eagle Farm, Queensland.

HER FACE AGLOW with the prevailing air of expectancy and excitement, Tessa Scott stood quietly at an observation window in the Brisbane Airport arrivals lounge, studying the throng of passengers now crossing the windswept tarmac from a recently landed Jumbo. Suddenly the girl's features creased in a radiant smile, as out of that multifarious crowd – for the most part so casually attired and understandably dishevelled – one figure had contrived to emerge clean-shaven, in a pin-stripe suit and guards' officer tie, with his boyish, breezy hair seemingly the only ruffled element in the package. He brushed it down with a hand as he entered the building.

'Hugh!' The man's face broke into a broad grin at the sound of Tessa's voice, and then he caught sight of her across the lounge, a stylishly cut trouser suit accentuating her height and slim figure, and shoulder length brown hair highlighting the exquisite planes of her face.

'Miss Muffet.' He spoke softly as they embraced.

'So good to see you, Hugh,' Tessa murmured into his shoulder. A moment later, the lawyer had slipped an arm proprietarily through the professor's and they were strolling off towards Customs.

'So you managed to get a direct flight to Brisbane – no Sydney stopover?' Tess assumed, as they neared the declarations area.

'Oh, Sydney can wait,' Hugh said dismissively. 'Far more interesting up here, by the sound of things. Any new developments?'

'Indeed there have been. Curious-er and curious-er, it all becomes.'

'Then the sooner we get on the trail the better, Tess. Oh, I took the liberty of arranging a hire car from the other end – thought an off-road vehicle might come in handy.'

'Good idea – my little car is a bit low for some of those tracks out there in the valley.'

Hugh now cleared his packages with Customs, with one long slim case requiring a little more paperwork than the rest, and they were soon stowing his luggage into the rear compartment of a long wheelbase Land Rover, delivered to the airport car-park by one of the international rental agencies. Late afternoon found Tess and Hugh walking arm in arm through the Brisbane botanical gardens, where the high notes of currawongs and the shriek of lorikeets vied for ascendancy over the rush of the westerly wind, the creak of swaying boughs and the chatter of flapping leaves. Refreshed and invigorated by their stroll, the pair then dined at dusk in a cosy inner-city restaurant, where they reminisced on old times and considered their tactics for the following day. It would be an early start for the Mirambeena district straight after breakfast, they decided, and an exploration of the old railway branch line to Rinehart's Ridge, particular the 'disused' level crossing where the *Diablo* had made its fiery entrance and Warren Schultz had vanished into the night.

At Tessa's invitation, Angela Reimann had agreed to meet the unofficial investigators at the crossing, at 2.30 on Saturday afternoon, in the hope that a return to the scene might jog the young woman's memory banks and potentially unlock some clue to the mystery. Hugh suggested that whilst they were *en route* to Mirambeena, a quick detour into the city of Ipswich might also pay dividends, provided, of course, that he could first succeed in contacting the steam enthusiast Maurice J. Arblaster to arrange a meeting. He had tried twice to phone Arblaster from England, he explained, after obtaining the man's company address from James Wyatt, but had been told by a secretary that Arblaster was away on business and would not be back until the weekend. The secretary had, however, provided Hugh with an after hours number, which he presently dialled at a public telephone just outside the restaurant.

'Arblaster!' The voice on the line was brusque, even aggressive. 'Who is it?'

'My apologies for disturbing you at home, Mr Arblaster,' the professor replied cheerily. 'My name's Hugh Bainbridge. A mutual acquaintance in England gave me your name and suggested that I look you up when I was out here.'

'Oh yeah, who's that?' The man's tone was cynical.

'A chap called James Wyatt – retired steam engineer.'

'Mmm. Vaguely remember the name. So, you're a steam train enthusiast.' The voice seemed to have mellowed slightly, though it was hardly friendly. 'Well, I'm sorry, Mr Bainbridge, but I really don't think I can be of any help to you. I've more or less given up any active involvement with steam trains – too many romantics and pie-eyed enthusiasts getting involved these days.'

'That's a shame,' Hugh said. 'I was heading west tomorrow and thought we might be able to meet somewhere and have a chat. I had hopes of tapping into your vast knowledge of steam technology.'

'Oh, I suppose you'll be heading out around Mirambeena, will you – to poke around some of the places where people have reportedly been abducted by this phantom express? It's all becoming a familiar story. You see, the truth is, Mr Bainbridge, that ever since this *Diablo* business broke, I've been besieged by every man and his dog, who invariably seem to expect that I should provide them with all the ins and outs of that antiquated, unstable monstrosity. Look, don't get me wrong – I'm a steam man and as Wyatt no doubt told you,

I'm on record as promoting a steam technology resurgence. I've even formed a group of like-minded souls – people who share my views of the advantages of steam – and that's why I allow my secretary to give out my after hours number. But you must understand that this group is not looking backward, to museum pieces like the *Diablo*. No sir, let me tell you, we're going forward.'

'It all sounds incredibly interesting, Mr Arblaster. You see, as keen as I am on the old stuff – the golden age of steam and all that – I'm also fascinated by the possibilities of building on past traditions; on modernising and updating, as it were, to create a future steam epoch. It's a pity we can't have a bit of a natter about it while I'm in the country; you know, share a few ideas.'

'Oh, all right then. I suppose I could spare an hour or so.' The gruff tones had softened a little. 'Look, why don't you call in tomorrow morning, at my office in Limestone Street. Say 9 am. Who knows? I might be able to tell you some interesting things about these Mirambeena train sightings too.'

'Thank you, Mr Arblaster. 9 o'clock it is then. I'll look forward to that.' Hugh hung up the telephone and turned with a quizzical smile to Tessa, who had been listening with interest.

'You old smoothie,' she laughed. 'Sounds as if he had a change of heart.'

'Hmm.' The professor looked thoughtful. 'He might turn out to be an interesting contact after all.

What surprised me was how rapidly he had the change of heart, unless he's just a moody customer.'

Chapter Seven
9am Saturday 16th July – Limestone Street, Ipswich, Queensland.

THE IDEA THAT Maurice J. Arblaster might conceal some sort of soft friendly centre beneath a blunt business exterior was quickly dispelled when Tessa and Hugh pulled up outside his investment consultancy offices at the appointed time on Saturday morning. The businessman had just arrived in his 450 SE Mercedes, and the sight of both Tessa's Fiat and Hugh's rented Land Rover pulling up at the kerb behind him was apparently enough to disturb his fragile equanimity and trigger one of his obviously mercurial mood swings.

'You didn't warn me that it was going to be a posse visiting, Mr Bainbridge?' Arblaster shouted as he made for the office door. Huge of stature and low of brow, he moved with a lumbering bear-like gait, pulling a door key from a flapping suit coat while grumbling over his shoulder at the pair of visitors, who followed cautiously while exchanging bemused glances.

'Have we never heard of the old saying "three's a crowd"?' Arblaster flung back the door and glanced back meaningly at Tessa. 'I don't care much for surprises, Bainbridge.'

'Now see here, old chap -' Hugh began, before Tessa moved to smooth things over.

'I could always go to a café and get a cup of tea,' she suggested, before Arblaster, clearly sensing that he had gone too far, relented.

'Oh, I don't suppose it matters. Now that you're here, one more won't make a difference. Steam enthusiast too, are we?' Again he looked at Tess.

'Tessa Scott,' the young woman said evenly, holding out her hand. 'I'm actually a lawyer by profession but yes, you could say that I've developed quite a keen interest in steam technology – in recent times anyway.'

'Fair enough.' Arblaster thrust out a ham-like hand. 'Look, I can certainly tell you a few things – stuff you mightn't know. First, however, I'll give you each a prospectus. That will explain to you where I'm coming from – and what I believe steam technology might be able to achieve in the future. It might also explain why I got out of hands-on engineering and into broad-based business consultancy. The other thing I'll do is tell you a bit about the past, the *Diablo* to be specific. It was a powerful engine, very advanced for its day, but it was built on too unstable a chassis and too narrow a frame.'

'That's interesting, Mr Arblaster,' Hugh said. 'And it confirms what James Wyatt suggested to me before I left England. He was kind enough to give me a demonstration, you know, using models.'

'Well now that you're here in this country, I'd suggest that you go out and see where the incident really happened. If you're going to the Mirambeena district, why not go out to Ziebarth's Bridge? It's only a few clicks from the crossing where that young Schultz fellow went missing a few weeks ago – well, that's if you believe that young woman's story. Some of us have difficulty with her tale, of course.'

'You mentioned last night that you might be able to tell me some interesting things about these recent train sightings,' Hugh prompted. 'Perhaps about that very incident reported by Miss Reimann?' The professor's gaze was wandering around the room as he spoke, his attention attracted by row upon row of photographs, which all seemed to feature Arblaster in the friendly company of an assortment of political leaders, entrepreneurs and captains of industry. Good advertising? Clever self-promotion? However one read the montage of press cuttings and publicity snaps, it was difficult to avoid the conclusion that Arblaster Consultancies had been involved, at least on the periphery, with an amazing sequence of investment coups, corporate raids and even the odd local or interstate political victory.

'I'll give you both my honest opinion,' Arblaster replied. 'I don't give that girl's story much credence at all, but a lot of people are claiming they've heard and seen a steam train recently. I'm more concerned with practical matters myself – some of which I'm now going to have to attend to – but if you've got a mind for mysteries, then go out this afternoon and check out the bridge I told you about. You might even still find evidence of the crash there – you know, bits of wreckage, a few souvenirs – perhaps something that will convince you, and others, that there's no *Diablo* still out there, plying the disused tracks of the Mirambeena Valley.'

'Hmm. I may just do that,' Hugh said airily. 'Ziebarth's Bridge you say?'

'That's it. A big curved concrete structure with a sixty foot drop into the creek. A tunnel right at one end of it. It's hard to miss if you travel east along the tracks from that now infamous disused crossing.'

'Well thank you, Mr Arblaster,' Hugh turned toward the door and exchanged meaningful glances with his colleague. 'There should be time this afternoon.'

'Yes, thank you, Mr Arblaster,' Tessa reiterated. 'We won't take up any more of your time.'

Saturday afternoon 16th July. Rinehart's Ridge, Mirambeena Valley, Queensland.

IT WAS JUST after 1pm and Professor Bainbridge's hired four-wheel drive was parked in a leafy glade next to a babbling stream, within a short distance of the humped up railway crossing where Warren Schultz had disappeared some three weeks before. A blanket was spread on the grass and in its centre a picnic hamper was surrendering an array of culinary delights purchased an hour earlier from a Mirambeena bakery and delicatessen. Magpies and butcher birds carolled in the trees, their notes blending with the steady splash and gurgle of the playful creek, as it tumbled over a low concrete crossing, then swirled away along a bed of moss-covered stepping stones.

'*By shallow rivers to whose falls, Melodious birds sing madrigals*'. Hugh murmured the words abstractedly, while he carefully placed some cheese and lettuce inside a bread roll.

'Yes, it is rather Marlowe-esque, isn't it?' Tess was seated opposite the professor, her black trousered legs extended to the edge of the blanket. She nibbled some ham and cheese and leaned back on her spare hand, letting her senses absorb to the full the tranquil ambience of the glade, the creek and the encircling bush. 'Or even Langland,' she mused. 'What are those lines from Piers Plowman?: *As I lay and lened and loked in the waters.*'

'*I slombred in a slepyng, it sweyued so merye.*' Hugh continued, recalling how apposite some earlier lines from the same poem had seemed on an English summer afternoon just a few days before. 'So here we are, Muffet, invoking the pastoral poets, and so far removed, it seems, from what we've come to investigate. It's frightfully difficult – on a day like this, in a spot like this – to conceive of fiery trains rushing through the night, picking up unwilling passengers.'

'Indeed it is,' said Tessa, pouring some tea from a flask into two cups. 'And yet we have Angela, and a range of other down-to-earth eye witnesses, who undoubtedly saw something convincingly like a train. What say we have this cuppa, and then go for an early reconnoitre along the tracks. We'll have more than an hour to spare before Miss Reimann gets here.'

'Good idea. Those first unvarnished impressions can often be instructive, before they're influenced by other people's observations.'

'Mmm – it's a bit like the first reading of a book, don't you think, before you go looking for what other readers or critics might have to say about it?'

SOME 20 MINUTES later, Tessa and Hugh had topped the nearby railway embankment and were strolling northward along a leaf-strewn, rust-pitted set of metals. The march was not a long one, for within a kilometre the tracks had ended in a mound of gravel, beyond which tangled scrub and vine had reclaimed their old dominion.

'According to an official I contacted at the railways department, this line was de-commissioned just after the war,' Tessa explained. 'Most of the track was torn up, but a section about five kilometres long was left intact, though disconnected from any other line.'

'They obviously thought it wasn't worth the costs that would have been involved in labour and machinery to go and rip it all up,' Hugh suggested. 'I wonder where this line went to originally.'

'Apparently it serviced some old coal mines, which petered out long ago,' Tess said. 'There were also a couple of whistle stop passenger stations along the track – including one at Rinehart' s Ridge – for the benefit of locals who wished to connect with the main inland line, which would in turn give them commuter access to Ipswich and towns like Layton and Mirambeena. The rise in popularity and greater affordability of cars after the war probably meant that branch line passengers eventually became few and far between.'

'We are left then with quite a logistical conundrum.' Hugh was gazing at the pile of rubble into which the tracks vanished, and at the acres of scrub beyond it. 'A train needs tracks on which to run. More so than any other form of transport, it sticks to the straight and narrow. Now how on earth did that steam train get onto this line – and off it?'

'Yes – and according to Angela's recollection of events, it was heading this way -north! After she left in Warren's car, the train must therefore have backed up this line, because, logically, it couldn't go any further in this direction.'

'Hmm. I wonder,' the professor mused, 'if somewhere along this track, someone might have temporarily re-instated a feeder line, leading off to one of the old abandoned coal mines.'

'A la *The Lost Special* by Conan Doyle?' Tessa replied, shaking her head. 'The problem with that theory is that the police apparently checked all along this line the next day, and they could find no trace of a feeder connection, or any signs of where one might have been temporarily set up. They also said there were no mine entrances along this remnant stretch of track – that they were all further north, beyond the scrub up there.'

Momentarily out of ideas, and aware that Angela Reimann was due to meet them in just over half an hour, the amateur investigators started back. The journey was an uneventful one until, as they neared the crossing, Tessa spotted something in the trackside grass and darted down the bank to retrieve it.

'Well, here's something the police missed,' she called out, holding aloft a Japanese style rubber sandal, of the type called a thong in Australia and a flip-flop in Britain. 'Mind you, so did we, on the outward walk.'

'Wasn't one of these found beside the tracks by Miss Reimann, on the night her beau went missing?' Hugh wondered. 'That makes the pair, then.'

'Yes.' Tess agreed. 'And both found in perfect

condition. It's a ghastly subject but no other items of apparel, or even remnants thereof, have been found.'

'And no real signs of a struggle – just the footwear left behind.'

'It's as if he was plucked up, by a giant hand.'

Pondering on Tessa's last remark, they both fell silent for a few moments, their gaze wandering up into the treetops, through the foliage and undergrowth surrounding the railway crossing and back down the quiet dirt road, still deserted save for a single sand-coloured Land Rover. The wind had now fallen and a mid-afternoon hush had descended on the forest; apart from an occasional nervous twitter and scuttle of birdlife in the lower bushes and lantana thickets, the whole area around the abandoned rail link was eerily quiet.

'To what purpose?' Hugh suddenly demanded. 'Why *are* these people simply vanishing, without trace? Could we be dealing with some secret *camorra* – diehard steam enthusiasts perhaps, out to make a point?'

'Some gang of terrorists?' Tessa wondered. 'Yet no demands have been made, of any kind. No claims of responsibility either.'

'Hmm. And it's a bit hard to imagine the Bader-Meinhoff, or the Red Brigade, or the Ananda Marga, running around in an antediluvian steam locomotive, isn't it?' Hugh paused and consulted his watch. 'Twenty three minutes to three. Is Miss

Reimann generally punctual, do you know?'

'She was certainly on time for our appointment at the coffee shop the other day,' Tessa recalled. 'I'll wait until three o'clock. If she hasn't arrived by then, I'll go back to the phone box in that little village, ring her home number in Mirambeena and try to find out if she's left yet.'

'Good idea. She may not have to cross any railway lines between Mirambeena and here, but it's best not to take chances.'

Three o'clock came and went, with still no sign of Angie Reimann.

'Do you mind waiting here, Hugh?' Tessa asked. 'In case she happens to turn up while I'm at the phone box.'

'Not at all,' Hugh replied, handing her the Land Rover keys. 'She may be completely thrown, if there's no one here to meet her.'

Tessa swung up into the driver's seat and was soon pushing the big, slow-revving four wheel drive up through the gears, pounding along the dirt road to the nearby village, where she alighted at the same public telephone box used by Angela Reimann on the night of Warren Schultz's disappearance. Less than fifteen minutes had elapsed before Hugh, waiting patiently in the shade of a large gum tree near the rail crossing, saw a cloud of dust which signalled the Land Rover's return. He opened the door to meet Tessa's anxious gaze.

'I spoke to Angie's father,' the lawyer explained.

'She apparently left her parent's home in Mirambeena around ten minutes to two.'

'Which should have placed her here well before the appointed time of two thirty,' Hugh calculated. 'Unless she's been delayed somewhere.'

'Mmm. Perhaps her car has broken down: a flat tyre or something. I think I'd better drive back towards town and see if I can find her. Do you still want to walk the line south of the crossing, out to Ziebarth's Bridge? I could come back later and pick you up.'

'Yes. I'd rather like to. I got the impression from Mr Arblaster that he would like me to do so, as well.'

'That may be a good reason not to go,' Tess said. 'Do you trust him?'

'Not a bit. But if he's got a trap in mind, I'd like to spring it, and possibly lure him, or his associates, out into the open.'

'Mmm. I'm not sure I like the idea of it. You may not actually get all the way out to Ziebarth's Bridge and back here before dark. And besides, even broad daylight may be no safeguard. The artist Frank Richards was convinced he saw the train during daylight hours.'

'Well, as you found no tracks around the setting of his painting, I think we have to assume that he was somehow mistaken. At any rate, I should surely be able to spot any train that tries to sneak up on me during the daytime.' Hugh paused to delve inside a jacket pocket. 'Now, according to this old map which you picked up from the railway authorities, if I keep walking south-eastwards past Ziebarth's Bridge, I should be within a couple of miles of Forest Junction, which I could easily make before dark. Would it be a bother for you to pick me up there, Muffet, rather than me walking back here?'

'No bother at all. As long as you're sure. It's a fair hike.'

'A mere bagatelle, my dear. What say I ring you at the motel, as soon as I get into Forest Junction?'

'That will be fine. Will you take anything with you?' Tessa glanced into the rear compartment of the four wheel drive.

'A water bottle, and *this*.' From a case in the back of the Land Rover, Hugh withdrew a sturdy alpenstock. 'What every serious walker needs,' he said airily.

Tess could not resist a broad smile. Save for an Akubra Plainsman hat, the tall lean figure in herringbone tweed jacket and knitted tie bore precious little resemblance to the average Australian bushwalker, yet that was the funny thing about Hugh: he should have come across as the very essence of the alien; the proverbial fish out of water, but somehow or other he didn't. Rather, he simply blended in, was always just himself, adding to the colour and diversity of the place, never challenging its traditions but adding to them. 'One of a kind'…

Tess held the thought as she leaned out the door, gave him a quick kiss on the cheek and started the engine.

'Well, I'd better get going then,' she said. 'Hopefully, I'll find this young woman has been delayed by nothing more serious than a flat battery, or some minor mechanical fault.'

Hugh touched a gentle hand on Tessa's shoulder before setting off. 'Do be careful, Miss Muffet,' he said softly.

TESSA WAS HURRYING the Land Rover along a narrow, bitumen surfaced laneway running between walls of scrub when her questing gaze discerned a small car in the distance, its nose angled downward on the thin strip of sloping roadside verdure. She braked cautiously, pulling up opposite the vehicle which she quickly recognised as the Toyota Corolla that Angie Reimann had parked outside the Mirambeena coffee shop on Thursday. The lawyer looked around warily, casting her eyes into the trees and undergrowth before alighting from the four wheel drive and crossing the road.

There was no one in the car, which was unlocked and keyless. Had the girl run out of petrol, or experienced engine problems perhaps, and decided to walk to the nearest habitation or garage?

A quick glance suggested otherwise. There were

other, larger tyre tracks on the grass ahead of the Corolla, along with smudged, intermingled footprints of at least three different sizes and shapes. One petite, patterned tread mark looked like the right sneaker size for Angela: the other shoe tracks were bulkier, one pair sporting the indented heel of a riding boot. Then came the clincher – a set of keys, including one with a Toyota badge, strewn in a clump of grass. Clearly there had been a struggle, as a result of which the girl had been overpowered and abducted. Heart pounding in spite of her outward calm, Tessa quickly used the key to open the Corolla's boot and, to her relief, found it empty.

'Right. Time to alert the official investigators.' Tessa locked the little car, walked across to Hugh's rented vehicle and gunned the engine. Twenty minutes later she pulled up in front of the Mirambeena police station and strode purposefully to the front desk. 'I want to report a missing person,' she told the young officer on duty. 'I have reason to believe she was abducted.'

'This isn't anything to do with a train, madam, is it?' The constable, whose name badge identified him as Ben Baker, shuffled in a slightly nervous way and looked over his shoulder. 'If it is, I should direct you to Inspector Jensen of the CIB. He's stationed here at present, and is personally handling all enquiries in regard to disappearances and –er – the train sightings.'

'Well, it may not be directly concerned with the

train,' Tessa explained. 'There does appear to be a connection though. Is the Inspector available now, because I must stress that the matter *is* urgent?'

'Did I hear my name mentioned?' The interjection came from a stocky, heavily-built man of around forty, who had emerged from an inner office to walk up beside the young constable and lean over the desk. He wore a tie knotted loosely, and the mass of black hair which spouted from his unbuttoned collar stood out in sharp contrast to the white of his shirt.

'The lady would like to report someone missing, Inspector,' the smartly uniformed officer explained.

'Gotcha, Charlie Brown: I'll take it from here,' the inspector grunted, before looking up at Tessa. 'Come through,' he said, lifting a panel in the desk and motioning to a chair as the girl followed him into his office. 'Now, tell me all your problems, sweetheart.'

'I'm not sure that I have any,' Tessa said, showing what she believed was admirable self-restraint. 'But one of my friends has. She was to meet me this afternoon out near Rinehart's Ridge – at the old railway crossing. When she didn't arrive, I went looking for her. I found her car, abandoned, and I could make out signs of a struggle. I believe she was abducted.'

'Fair dinkum? Maybe she just left the car and went for a walk – did you think about that?' The detective was leaning across his desk, his face a sardonic mask.

'After throwing her keys in the grass?' Tessa replied, dangling Angela's key-ring.

'She mighta dropped 'em.'

'There were other fresh tracks nearby – of a large vehicle and at least two more people.'

'For a fancy city lawyer, you make a pretty good black-tracker, eh?' The man actually guffawed. 'Or maybe you see yourself as a female Sherlock Holmes? You're a bit young yet for Miss Marple.'

'How do you know who, or what, I am?' Tessa demanded. 'I haven't as yet been given the opportunity to provide my name or address – which seems, if I may so, something of an oversight at the start of a police investigation. Do you intend to take a formal statement of interview?'

'No need to get excited, sweetheart. I make it my business to know who's poking around the place – copper's keen sense o' smell, you know.' The man scratched the top of his nose meaningly. 'Now, if you're representing that Reimann girl, let me give you a few informal facts. I don't trust her one little bit. I think she could have done her boyfriend in, and just possibly she's now staged her own disappearance. As for these other people who claim to have seen a train, I think they're all either delusional or maybe they've had a drop too much of the old amber fluid.'

'I see, Inspector. Well, if that sort of blanket

judgment is any indication of your investigative acumen, it's hardly surprising that you haven't yet enjoyed much success with the case.'

'Now see here, missy.' The detective's face reddened deeply as he replied. 'I'll give you some free advice. Why don't you just head back to Mexico: go home and play your Trixie Belden games in the socialist South. We've got a crack CIB team here with feelers out on the whole thing. The last thing we'll wear is some dolly bird Sydney lawyer coming up here and poking her beak in where it isn't wanted.'

'I'd like to know the name of your superior, Inspector,' Tessa replied coolly. 'And also, the person who is in charge of this station.'

'Oh, don't come that line, sweetie,' the man chuckled. 'My boss back in Brissie is, let's just say, very supportive of the way I'm handling things out here. You see, these local yokels are all right when it comes to traffic enforcement and delivery of summonses, but they know bugger-all about criminal investigation. We've had a bit of an internal shake-up, both here and down at headquarters. A few internal transfers; some new blokes on the beat here in town; a new sergeant in charge o' the uniformed guys. Bit of a spring clean, you might say.'

'I see.'

'Yeah.' The inspector winked and leered across the table. 'So, if you're thinking of approaching any other officers, just keep this in mind: you must know the Yank expression 'good cop, bad cop' – well, it sort of applies around here, except that it's pretty hard to know who the good guys actually are these days. You get my drift?'

'I believe I do, yes.'

'So, gorgeous – my advice, at the end of our *informal* interview, is the same as when I started. Go home!'

'So, you're running me out of town, sheriff?' Tessa said dryly.

'Call it what you like. Let's just say that I'd prefer not to see you, or your Pommy boyfriend, around here for too long.'

Tessa's surprise at the latter remark must have registered on her face, despite her best efforts, because the policeman leaned forward with an arrogant smirk. 'Know this, sweetie: between us and Special Branch, and those in the know at headquarters, we've got our fingers on the pulse of this whole valley. If a dog farts up one of these back roads, I'll soon get to hear about it.'

'Don't you still require a warrant to tap telephones?'

'Whoa! Who said anything about telephones? Hey Jimbo!' The inspector shouted into an adjoining room. 'Did I say anything about telephones?'

'Never heard a thing, boss.' A uniformed officer – slightly older and more heavily built than the one at the front desk – now slouched in to lean on the table in front of Tessa's chair. 'Phones, you say? Nah, never heard you mention phones.'

The new arrival wore a senior constable's insignia on his uniform, although in sharp contrast to young Ben Baker, his collar was open, his shirt looked unironed and his elastic-sided boots, with their chunky heels, looked decidedly non-regulation.

'Good afternoon then, Inspector,' Tessa said, starting toward the door. 'I won't say it's been a pleasure, but it's been quite informative in its own way. Oh, don't get up. I'll find my own way out.'

The Westerly wind had freshened when Tessa walked outside the station and the position of the sun suggested that a cold night was no more than an hour away. She slipped on a jacket from the recesses of the Land Rover and drove off to the home of Angela Reimann's parents. Somehow, it came as no surprise to find the front door askew on its hinges, no one at home in the house and a set of large tyre tracks in the driveway. A friendly neighbour said he had heard a few bangs and crashes, had assumed that the Reimanns had hired some weekend handymen for house repairs, and had therefore taken little notice of the occupants of a Ford F100 truck which had entered the driveway and left in 'a bit of a hurry'.

Based on her recent encounter with Inspector Jensen and 'Jimbo', Tessa could see little point in again contacting the police. Apart from the wrecked door, there appeared to be no overt signs of violence, so the most prudent course appeared to be to return to the Bluegum Motel, where earlier in the day she had left the Fiat. There, securely ensconced in her room, she made a cup of tea, put up her feet and resolved to simply ponder the situation until she received a phone call from Hugh.

Chapter Eight
Late afternoon, Saturday 16th July

APART FROM AN occasional buffet of wind in the clearings, Professor Hugh Bainbridge was enjoying his walk along the old abandoned railway line that still stretched between Rinehart's Ridge and Ziebarth's Bridge. The atmosphere was one of almost jaunty dilapidation, with a bouncy Nature determinedly re-asserting itself at every turn. Much of the track was leafy and shaded, and those sections exposed to full sunlight were often overgrown with clumps of grass, weeds and bramble. Here and there he passed tumbledown siding sheds, surrounded by lantana and overgrown by scrub vines. There were places too where rotting wooden sleepers no longer supported the rusting metals, and to Hugh it seemed an utter mystery how any heavy locomotive with carriages in tow could have travelled this way in recent times. He poked with his alpenstock at Scotch thistles thrusting up between yawning seams in the rails, and wondered.

It was twenty to five when the Oxford don at last marched out of a cavern of over-hanging scrub and saw before him a high-arched railway bridge, spanning a yawning gorge between two rocky hillsides. The sun was already dipping down onto the ranges to his right, highlighting the twin glistening bands of the track before they speared into a long, dank tunnel. For several minutes Hugh stood, eyeing off the length of the bridge and looking out over the inter-lacing network of narrow streams which divided and re-converged around boulders and tiny islets all along the river bed. A freshet caused by an un-seasonal downpour a few weeks earlier had left several deep, stagnant pools shimmering below muddy, reed-choked banks but the running water was mostly shallow, coursing over ancient pathways of pebbles and gravel. In several places, large eucalypts and willow trees overhung the banks, while an occasional ironbark or blue gum thrust out great clawing arms as if to challenge the steel and concrete battlements of the bridge.

'Hmm. It does look a trifle exposed out there,' Hugh soliloquised. 'Still, one should surely get wind of an approaching train while it's still well back in the tunnel: that should give a fellow enough time either to beat a hasty retreat, or to make a dash for that safety platform close to the tunnel mouth. Oh well, on with it then: nothing ventured, nothing gained, and all that rot.'

So steeling himself, the professor set off, suppressing with great difficulty his dread of heights as he walked along the narrow super-structure, with its giddying lack of guard-rails and its kaleidoscopic views of distant riverbed between the cross girders. He advanced with trepidation, using the alpenstock to steady himself, though several times he almost froze in his tracks, as vertigo attacked his knees and fear clutched at the pit of his stomach. Mountains and hills he loved, but a sheer dizzying drop like this was pure torture.

'Hmm. Not much fun at all,' he mused, trying to keep his gaze fixed straight ahead as rigidly as possible, all the while becoming acutely aware that acrophobia was not the sole cause of his unease. That black tunnel mouth had leered at him from the outset, and now there seemed an almost spell-like quality about it, as if it were reeling him in, enchanting the wayward foot traveller into its maw. He halted suddenly in the middle of the bridge, peering into the opening, unsure if his eyes were playing him false.

What on earth? Amid the shadows and gloom of that cavernous aperture, there now appeared to be something even blacker – a vast, menacing entity, waiting to pounce. A sudden rumble shook the bridge, while within the tunnel a huge, tank-like profile was delineated by red licks of flame and a fierce subterranean glow. A thunderous *whoosh* echoed and re-echoed around the hillsides, as a great swathe of light lanced out across the bridge from the cavern entrance, to dissipate amid the fading rays of the afternoon sun. Oblivious to the drop below, Hugh Bainbridge turned on his heel and fled.

There was a quarter of the bridge left to run when the professor felt the *Diablo*'s hot breath at his back. Clearly, it was impossible to outrun the train – or whatever this shrieking, clanking monstrosity really was. Instead, Bainbridge turned sideways and leaped from the bridge. His hands clawed wildly for the topmost branches of a riverbank gum tree, caught hold, and for an instant he dangled, suspended at full arm's stretch from a creaking bough. Shoulder and arm muscles straining, Hugh chanced a direct downward glance, into a darkly glistening pool situated beneath an overhanging, grass-covered creek bank. Slowly, one hand after the other, he began edging in toward the tree trunk; until suddenly, with a crack like a gunshot, the branch gave way.

For a moment Hugh felt that he was plummeting through a horizontal forest. While his flailing arms clutched madly for a handhold, a myriad small branches and leafy twigs snatched and clawed at the folds of his tweed jacket and trousers, each limb snapping, folding over or otherwise collapsing beneath his weight but all assisting in retarding his descent. Oblivious to abrasions and bumps, the don twisted desperately as he fell, until at last, using an adaptation of a martial arts manoeuvre that Westmead had once demonstrated, he looped his arms around one of the river gum's giant lower branches and swung up his legs. It took him several seconds to realise that he had stopped falling.

Once again Bainbridge had time to catch his

breath and take stock of his position. He was now some six metres above the creek bank – still too far to fall onto solid ground – and was upside down like a sloth, gripping the branch with both hands and feet. He glanced upward, and discerned the *Diablo*, seemingly frustrated in its forward charge, now reversing back across the bridge till it was positioned above him. With the fading afternoon sun lending it an ethereal radiance, it seemed to hover and dance just above the rails, while the professor's eyes blinked in utter disbelief. With no easy way down and once more feeling very exposed, Hugh began to wriggle out along the bough, until at last he was clear of the bank and above the pool.

At this point, Bainbridge suddenly felt his nostrils assailed by a strangely caustic odour and glancing up again he detected a cloud of vapour, wafting toward him from the menacing black and red presence on the bridge overhead. The smell was hard to define but it was certainly nothing like coal soot.

'What on earth?' This new development was more than enough for the professor. He would cast his fate to the waters, and hope to goodness they were deep enough.

'Cheerio then,' he yelled defiantly. 'Can't afford to hang about like thi-is!' His voice trailed off as he simply let go of the branch and plummeted, twisting like a madman in mid-air so as to avoid hitting the stagnant pool in a potentially disastrous backward or forward flop. Somehow he managed to cleave the water with both hands first, in a semblance of a dive, and a few seconds later he had safely re-surfaced, striking out immediately for solid ground.

The *Diablo*, hissing and puffing its apparent frustration, backed up towards its tunnel lair, as Professor Bainbridge, in clothes now both saturated and tattered beyond recognition, paused only to retrieve his wildly flung alpenstock before darting across the river bed and into the cover of some scrub.

WITHIN THE THICK belt of scrub covering the hillside to the east of Ziebarth's Bridge, Hugh Bainbridge found that night had already fallen. The most practical route on offer if he wished to stay hidden was upward via a vegetation-choked gully, but the darkness made progress frustratingly slow, and there were hazards aplenty. While his alpenstock came in handy for fending aside lianas and lantana, it could not prevent his hand once or twice coming into painful contact with a stinging tree, a plant he would have seen and recognised had the light been good. Such mishaps notwithstanding, the professor was grateful for the all-enveloping cover the scrub provided, and when at last he found himself cresting the rise with another vine-knotted gully plunging downhill before him, he was sure he was moving in the right direction to intersect with the road to Forest Junction.

Despite the increasing darkness, and the concomitant risks of blundering into things, the scrub now seemed warm and inviting, with its friendly smell of leafage and its protection from the chill south-westerly wind. It was a haven from the outside world – no longer a *wild wood* this – and it was like losing a security blanket when Hugh suddenly broke forth into an open grassy paddock.

A mob of roan and white cattle raised their heads from grazing long enough to cast a curious eye at the stranger as he made his way across their domain to a barbed wire fence and a dusty track that shimmered white in the gathering dusk.

'This then must be my road,' announced Hugh loftily. 'I dare say it intersects somewhere with one of the main bituminised thoroughfares leading to Forest Junction or Mirambeena.'

It wasn't a bad evening for a stroll, he reflected, although the confounded wind had freshened up again, its freezing tentacles making life just a little uncomfortable for a traveller in squelching boots and soggy clothing. Still, the further he tramped along this quiet country lane, the dryer he became, and the less chance there seemed to be of encountering some rampant, vengeful locomotive. While it was hard to resist the occasional backward glance, and prudence made him carefully peruse every shadow cast by the gum trees ahead, it appeared more and more likely to the professor that he had thrown off his pursuers.

A *very* quiet laneway, this. Apart from a gambolling hare and, later on, a wallaby that separated itself from the roadside shadows to thump off up the increasingly moonlit track, Hugh discerned no signs of activity whatsoever, until quite unexpectedly the soft yellow light of a public telephone box winked happily into view. The professor quickened his pace and in short order he was ensconced inside the welcoming glass-and-wooden structure, plunging coins into a slot and dialling the number of the Bluegum Motel. It was a relief to hear Tessa's cheerful, mellifluous voice at the other end of the line.

'Hugh, where are you? Are you alright?'

'Miss Muffet! Fine, thank you. Though I must say that I've had rather an eventful afternoon. Is everything alright with you?'

'Perfect. Though I've become very concerned about young Angela. I found her car, abandoned on the side of the road, and on top of that her parents now seem to have gone missing from their home. I'm certain they've all been kidnapped.'

'You've been to the police?'

'Yes. Not much satisfaction there, I'm afraid. It's probably best if I don't go into that issue right now – I'll explain when I pick you up.'

'Right you are. Now, I'm at a place called, let me

see –' Hugh peered out on to the rustic contours of an old weatherboard building, the bulb inside the phone box providing just sufficient light to delineate the lettering on a faded hoarding. '*Hauser's General Store and Post Office, Schaefer's Grove,*' he read aloud. '*KR Darling Downs Smallgoods, Kirks' Soft Drinks, Coca Cola.* However, they don't appear to be selling any of that just at present. Very quiet, on this front.'

Indeed, the total lack of lighting within the shop seemed to suggest that Saturday evenings were not regarded as prime trading hours at Schaefer's Grove; either that, or the business was permanently closed. The fact that no light burned in the living quarters at the back of the premises implied strongly that the place was unoccupied, or perhaps the householders were simply out playing bingo.

'I know where that place is,' Tessa said. 'It's not too far from Forest Junction. Wait right there. I'm coming to get you.'

'Thank you, Tessa. I'll stay put then. Now, what the dickens? Hold on – something a bit rum here.' Hugh's voice sounded baffled. The soft lighting inside the old phone booth was somehow increasing in intensity. The rising moon? … the headlights of a car approaching down the laneway? Surely it must be the latter. Bainbridge turned to peer out.

Suddenly the night dissolved in a brilliant yellow explosion of light. It seemed to pour from the brow of a vast metallic face, which rushed from the darkness toward the phone box, shrieking and hissing demoniacally. Half-blinded, Hugh could scarcely believe what any of his senses suggested. A train? …without tracks? Yes – unmistakably it was – a gleaming black and scarlet juggernaut, boring down with unstoppable fury upon this fragile, glowing cage, and the flailing desperate figure, trapped inside like a fly in a bottle.

On the other end of the phone line, Tessa heard a thunderous, splintering crash. She dropped the receiver onto the bedside handset, leaped to her feet and raced out through the motel room door. In an instant the Fiat coupe had snarled into action and with a screech from the rear tyres the young lawyer was tearing down the driveway and out onto the main street of Mirambeena, en route to the Forest Junction turnoff.

IT WAS A WILD yet inspired drive for Tessa and her Fiat, on that windy July night. The young woman's hands moved gently and sparingly at the wheel, her left dropping from time to time to flick the gear lever into a different plane, while her feet danced over clutch, brake and accelerator pedals with such harmony that the car never deviated as much as an inch from the line she willed it to trace. And all the while the miles were gobbled at a rate which drivers of lesser skill, in more pedestrian machinery, would have found difficult to comprehend. All up it was a precision display, which transported Tessa in record time to the little township of Forest Junction, and beyond that to an intersection signposted to Schaefer's Grove.

Turning down the narrow side road, the lawyer steered a brisk course between moonlit fields of potatoes and shimmering pastures of lucerne, her gaze questing earnestly for the glow of a village telephone box. It was a rather different light which suddenly arrested her attention, however – a single, blindingly powerful headlamp, spearing directly towards her – and behind that light were some two hundred tons of steam locomotive!

Tessa flicked the steering wheel to the left … the train tracked right, as if to meet her. She veered to the right, and sure enough, the great lumbering leviathan steamed across to intersect with her new path. There seemed to be only one course of action left, one which relied strongly on the rational laws of physics: however this monstrosity was constructed, Tessa reasoned swiftly, its sheer bulk should prevent it from changing direction as quickly as her diminutive coupe. She floored the throttle, shooting straight toward the on-rushing face of the locomotive.

The hideous yellow beam of the train's headlight flooded across the car's bonnet and through the low slung windscreen. Tessa had to drop her gaze low to avoid being blinded, but still she powered on.

'Now!' At the last minute, the girl whipped the wood-rimmed steering wheel to the left, aiming for a gap of perhaps eight to ten feet between the steaming flanks of the *Diablo* and the unyielding wooden posts and taut barbed wire of a farmer's fence.

Whether the train once more attempted to change direction, Tessa could not be sure. Her full concentration was on keeping the car steady along the slippery verge, and all she caught was a mere peripheral glimpse of a gleaming red-streaked coal tender with a couple of trailing wooden carriages, flashing past. An instant later, the girl had fish-tailed the Fiat back onto the road, heaving a sigh of relief as the fiery apparition in her rear-view mirror receded into the distance. Whatever motive force or bizarre traction system it possessed, the train was clearly not stopping, or turning around in pursuit. Within seconds, the night had swallowed up every sign of its passage.

Just half a kilometre further on, Tessa brought her car to a halt beside the darkened outlines of a general store, where a narrow dirt laneway intersected with the bitumen road she had been following. But where was Hugh's telephone box?

The wash of the Fiat's headlamps soon told the story. Where once a bright red telephone cabinet had stood proudly erect by the roadside, a thousand glass shards, shattered fragments of matchwood and slivers of Bakelite were all that remained, littering the grass verge and spilling out across the laneway.

Tessa peered around anxiously. The wan glow of moon and starlight invested the scene with an air of edgy surrealism. Something that looked like an eye, winking hideously at her from beneath a splintered pane of glass, revealed itself as a coat sleeve button when she knelt to inspect it.

And was that? Yes, a strip of tweed cloth was fluttering from a metal triangle that had once served as a door hinge.

'Hugh!' the girl called out, unable to suppress the tremble in her voice. 'Hugh, where are you?' She rushed off down the laneway, her gaze darting left and right. Fifty metres; a hundred – nothing! Until suddenly – in the middle of a moonlit paddock – a sudden movement seized her attention. Looped through the lower framework of a Southern Cross windmill, the tattered remains of a tweed jacket were flapping gently in the breeze.

Darting between the strands of a barbed wire fence, Tessa broke into a run across the field. She gave a shout of joy as she made out the yawning aperture of a well beneath the windmill, and beside it, planted like a flagpole in the muddy overspill of a cattle trough, stood Hugh Bainbridge's alpenstock.

'Miss Muffet! Is that you?' The voice echoed up to Tessa from the depths, resounding off foot after foot of well casing. 'I say, old thing: these Aussie wells of yours are a jolly sight harder to get out of than they are to get into.'

'Hugh! Hugh, are you alright? Did you drop all the way down there?'

'No. Only about the last eight or ten feet. There's a ladder of sorts higher up, but the lower rungs are rotten. They broke away under me. Perhaps I should go on a diet – that's the second lot of timber that's collapsed under my weight today.'

'You poor thing. Now, let me see. How on earth are we going to get you out of there?'

'Well, I'm treading water at the moment, although I can almost touch bottom. There's nothing of any use down here, by the look of it. I don't suppose there's any rope or chain to be had up there, is there?' Hugh's view as he gazed upward was a distant circle of starlight, onto which the silhouette of Tessa's head and shoulders was now superimposed. To the professor's astonishment however, another shape was insinuating itself into the picture – a baleful outline behind and above the girl, with long limbs that clawed down at her.

'Muffet – look out!' Hugh shouted. As two great arms looped around her, Tessa relaxed in their grip; then drove her elbow back into her attacker's midriff. The man grunted, losing his hold as the girl rounded on him and slammed home a right cross to his jaw. As her assailant staggered backward, Tessa darted after him, and in the moonlight recognised the face of Jimbo, the ostensible senior constable at the Mirambeena police station. For a moment, the lawyer hesitated and Jimbo seized the opportunity to pull a small knife from his jacket pocket, flick it open and strike at her.

Any thought that this might be some legitimate officer of the law now vanished from Tessa's mind, as she twisted sideways out of harm's way, grabbed the man's outstretched arm and flung him face first to the ground. Before he could even think of regaining his feet, she had brought down her extended hand across the back of his neck, and Jimbo collapsed in a soporific swoon. An instant later, to Hugh's enormous relief, Tessa was leaning back over the well top.

'Now, where were we?' she called out cheerily. 'Ah yes; something to help you climb out of there, that's the issue.'

'Miss Muffet, are you alright?' Hugh called back. 'What on earth was that all about?'

'Believe it or not, that was a member of the local constabulary – well, in theory at least. I'm not sure what it was all about, but I'm assuming that he wasn't trying to take me into custody – unless flick knives have suddenly become a legitimate part of arrest procedure.'

'Flick knives?' Hugh's voice was aghast. 'The man has to be an impostor, or a bent copper perhaps. I gather you've subdued him for the present?'

'He appears to be sleeping soundly, for the moment.' Tessa was peering around earnestly as she spoke. 'Now let me see – there's something over in that cultivation that might help. Hold on: I'll be right back.'

The young woman was as good as her word. In a moment she had returned, with the considerable length of an irrigation pipe hoisted over her shoulder.

'I'll have to be careful how I lower this thing down,' she called out. 'I'll swing it upright, feed one end into the hole and then just lower it as far as I can. I'm sure it won't reach all the way down to you, so I'll have to eventually drop it, I'm afraid. Do you think you can stay clear of it, by hugging the wall?'

'A mere bagatelle, Tess,' the professor assured her. 'Lower away: I'll keep out of harm's way.'

Down the metal tubing came, dangling against the well casing, with Tessa at full stretch clinging to the uppermost end; until at last the lower end of the pipe came to a stop, still a good fifteen feet above the waterline.

'Let it go, my dear,' Hugh called up brightly. 'I'll take my chances.' Tessa did, and the pipe speared down into the depths, breaking the surface a couple of feet from Hugh, who had been observing its progress and trajectory keenly, his back pressed firmly against the opposite side of the well.

'Well done, Muffet,' Hugh cried. 'A palpable hit! Now, let's see if one can clamber or shin up the confounded thing.' Paddling across to the pipe, the professor looped his arms and legs awkwardly around it and started hauling himself up out of the water. Grinning slightly in spite of herself at the grunts and occasional epithets which echoed up from the well, Tessa alternated between cautious glances in the direction of Jimbo's sprawled figure, and anxious downward peeks to check on Hugh's progress. Her concern mounted as the professor swung himself sideways and gingerly transferred his weight from the pipe to the remains of the safety ladder. When at last she could see him clearly, approaching confidently hand over hand up the final few rungs to the top, she heaved a sigh of relief.

For Hugh, the view as he ascended was one of the most welcome he could ever recall – that beaming face, with its frame of silky brown hair and its backdrop of soft moonlight, and now a steady hand reaching out to him. Their eyes met, negating speech, and a moment later they were embracing.

'I'm terribly sorry, Miss Muffet,' Hugh said at last. 'But I am just a little damp – well, more than a little actually. And I fear that your clothes will be soaked now as well.'

'A mere bagatelle,' Tessa smiled. Her expression changed to one of concern as she looked more closely at his face. 'You poor dear, you *are* hurt. Your forehead's been cut.'

'Oh, a mere trifle, my dear. Had an argument with a gum tree, don't you know? Actually, it's just as well the branches did claw at me and slow my descent, although they made a frightful mess of my old tweed jacket.' Hugh gestured at the badly torn garment fluttering nearby, and winced.

'Yes, you might need a change of attire soon, I think,' Tess allowed. 'You've certainly been through the mill, haven't you? And no pun intended.'

'I'll tell you all about it later, but – hello, what's this? Our captive's doing a runner.' Hugh was now looking past Tessa, in the direction of the laneway, where the blare of a car horn and a flash of headlights was directing the rushing boots of Jimbo. The roar of a powerful engine, departing in an acrid cloud of dust, drifted back to the lawyer and the don as they raced across the paddock in pursuit.

'V8, judging by the engine note,' Hugh panted.

'Mercedes, by the look of those tail-lights,' Tessa suggested.

'450SE, or I miss my guess.'

'Like the one our friend Arblaster drives.'

'So: he sets me up for a rendezvous with the train, and now he's poking about trying to ascertain where I've bolted to. He's our man and no mistake – or one of them!'

'Yes,' agreed Tessa. 'And he obviously has connections with these dodgy policemen.'

'He has connections with just about everybody, judging by the walls of his office.'

'It's a big conspiracy, Hugh,' Tessa said thoughtfully, as she got through the fence. 'Just how far the tentacles reach is hard to say, but I'm starting to think that a certain egregious police inspector, whose acquaintance I made this afternoon, might not have been exaggerating when he said they had feelers everywhere.'

'Hmm. Makes it jolly hard to know whom to trust – and hard to know where to take our little investigation from here.'

'Well, I think the first priority is to get you back to the motel, so that you can have a warm shower and a change of clothes. You must be nearly frozen, poor thing. After that, we can discuss tactics.'

'You're right, of course.' Hugh paused a moment to survey the paddock. 'All right, I've grabbed the old alpenstock and what's left of the coat. Unfortunately, the Akubra went west somewhere near Ziebarth's Bridge, so I shall have to replace that trusty chapeau at some point. Which way to your car, Tess?'

'I left it near the store, and that wrecked phone box. I have to say that shattered cabinet gave me some anxious moments, Hugh – though it must have been a lot worse for you, when it was all going on. What happened exactly, and how on earth did you end up in that well?'

'I'm not ashamed to admit that I was taking refuge down there,' Hugh explained as they jogged along the laneway towards the rustic profile of Hauser's corner store. 'I only barely made it out of the phone box – after catching my coat sleeve on the door – before the loco ploughed into it and sent timber and glass pluming fifty feet into the air. I then found myself pursued across a paddock – and all this by a train that doesn't require tracks.'

'Well, this is all reassuring, in a way,' Tessa replied. 'Now we've both seen it at first hand. We know for a fact that it exists and that it doesn't have to stay on metal lines. At first I thought I might have been hallucinating, after the darn thing nearly ran me off the road. That happened just a few minutes before I arrived here – it must have been leaving the scene after its failed attempt at running you down.'

'Yes. The whole thing is mind boggling. But taking up your point, Tess, we've now established beyond any doubt the credibility of witnesses such as Angela Reimann and that artist chappie. What we still don't know, of course, is *how* this train does what it does – its method of propulsion; how its traction and suspension system work; how it can travel on roads and across fields without bogging down.'

'And *why* it does all these things? *Why* all these mysterious disappearances, without so much as a trace, or the hint of a motive? Arblaster is surely too hard-nosed a businessman to be caught up in some stunt to promote the cause of steam.'

'No, he's playing some deeper game, I'm willing to wager. I wonder if there's anything to be gleaned by re-reading that prospectus of his, although it seemed quite a nebulous document at first glance.' Hugh's teeth were chattering by the time they reached the old corner shop, where the couple quickly took refuge from the icy wind inside the cosy confines of Tessa's Fiat. A moment later they were hurrying back towards Mirambeena, with the heater at full blast and the professor ensconced in the welcome folds of a travel blanket.

'That was an exquisite idea to use the alpenstock and jacket to signal your location,' Tess laughed. 'Was the train right behind you at the time?'

'It was getting jolly close. The glare of its headlight was all around me just before I got into the well. Thinking back, I might have been an easy target down there, but at the time all I could think of was getting away from that pursuing monstrosity. I suppose at that stage I even harboured doubts as to whether the *Diablo* was humanly guided, though it clearly must have been. I'm not sure why they abandoned the chase, but I could hear a couple of vehicles moving around nearby soon after I fell into the water. One sounded like a lorry rumbling slowly along the dirt road – a farmer perhaps – so they might have thought there were too many witnesses about to risk stopping the train and dealing further with me. Either that, or they had another job somewhere else. Perhaps, after seeing me in the phone box, they guessed that you'd be coming, and went back deliberately to run you off the road.'

'It might not have been a guess,' Tessa said. 'I believe the phone in my motel room has been bugged, because the police inspector I spoke to this afternoon seemed to know a great deal about our movements. Someone listening in tonight could easily have contacted your pursuers by CB radio, or some sort of field communication equipment.'

'Hmm. They seem to be holding a lot of the cards, Muffet.' Hugh gazed out thoughtfully at the moonlit farm paddocks, flashing past on either side of the little Italian car, and wondered aloud. 'Now, there's another strange thing about the *Diablo* – it leaves no breaks in fences.'

'Yes. Amazing, isn't it? Nor does it leave tracks of any kind; no marks on the ground at all. It's almost as if we *are* dealing with some sort of infernal machine: something that floats around and simply wafts people up.'

'Some type of hovering system,' Hugh suggested. 'It has to be.'

‘A cushion of air, like a hovercraft?’

‘Or a cushion of steam perhaps – I wonder if that’s feasible. One thing I can vouch for is that it does an exceptional amount of hissing, accompanied by the usual clanking noises of rolling stock.’

‘Did you actually see any people in the train, Hugh – either in the loco, or the carriages?’

‘No, strangely enough. Of course, in the most recent escapade, the headlight virtually blinded me and I hardly looked back after I started running. But earlier on, when there was still a bit of light about and I was dangling from a tree branch next to Ziebarth’s Bridge, I had a reasonable view of the train as it shunted backwards above me. The problem then, however, was that it appeared to be shimmering and floating in the afternoon light – rather surreal in a sense – and I could discern no human forms at all.’

‘I was just thinking back on what Angie told me – about figures leaping around in the cab, and one huge man getting ready to jump; or at least leaning forward toward the doorway.’

‘Perhaps getting ready to scoop somebody up?’ Hugh suggested. ‘I wonder: Arblaster’s a very big chap, as I recall.’

‘Mmm. I suppose his mate Jimbo is a fair size too. So, for that matter, is the police inspector – Jensen – but it all gets back to that connection, doesn’t it? And we don’t know how far those connections extend. There seems little point in approaching the police again, when we don't know who's corrupt and who isn't. And from what Jensen said, they could have informants all around the district.'

'We're going to have to tread very carefully, Muffet.'

'I think perhaps we should go home,' Tessa announced after a thoughtful pause.

'Eh?' Hugh looked askance at his companion.

'At least, that's what we let Jensen, Arblaster, Jimbo *et al* think. Let them believe that they *have* run us out of town, but in reality we simply go into hiding – vanish to some bolt hole, from which we can conduct our investigation in a more discreet manner.'

'Somewhere back in the scrub, away from the prying gaze of passing traffic?'

'Exactly,' Tess smiled, her face aglow in the soft lights of the instrument panel. 'Ah – *once again, do I behold these steep and lofty cliffs...*'

That on a wild secluded scene impress ...
Thoughts of more deep seclusion.

'Aha,' the professor grinned. 'Wordsworth is apposite, as always. I think we both know just such a place, Tess – the good old lean-to, what?'

'You know, it's funny. Dad mentioned on the way up here that the old hut would be a good spot for some rest and recreation. I'm not sure if he had it in mind as a hide-out exactly, but it should be isolated enough for our purposes.'

'Quite,' said Hugh. 'Yet happily, its seclusion is not absolute. There are neighbours in those hills, as I recall – solid, dependable, and thoroughly incorruptible neighbours, or I miss my guess.'

'You're thinking of the Steiler brothers, no doubt.' Tessa laughed, as thoughts came flooding back of their stay in the region last year, and two men who had helped to unravel a very different sort of mystery. 'All I can say is, pity help the would-be standover merchant who tries to lean on, or recruit, those siblings.'

'And that would apply to a few others, I'll wager, from around those scrubby gullies. Despite what your police inspector says, I don't see the farmers of Junction Ridge being any pushover.'

'Indeed. Although I suppose it depends on what sort of coercion has been brought to bear. Threats against family members, other loved ones, livelihood and property can often force good people to toe the line, at least temporarily. We'll have to be very careful who we approach.'

'I suppose the first task is to thoroughly convince them that we've left town. That may be no easy task, considering the close tabs they're keeping on us.'

'Indeed. As I said earlier, it would seem they've been monitoring our activities very closely, right down to tapping the motel telephone system.'

'Perhaps we can use that to our advantage, Tess. Suppose I make a phone call tonight to my colleague and co-writer in Sydney, and explain that over the next couple of weeks, I'll be doing some research on Paterson, Lawson and Co. around country New South Wales. She's a good sport and she's bound to take it well when I eventually do catch up with her and explain the circumstances. I'll also ring the car rental agency at the airport and tell them that I want to return the Land Rover in Sydney.'

'Aha!' Tessa nodded in agreement. 'And then check out of the motel rooms and leave town in full daylight tomorrow, just to ensure that our departure is well and truly noted? We can double back later.'

'I was wondering if we could even get off to an early start – that would seem like a logical approach for a couple of travellers with a long journey in front of them. We should notice the carlights of any spies who might be about and, just as importantly, they should see us leave and head south toward the New England Highway. Once we're sure that we're not being followed, however, we can cut across to Junction Ridge via one of those good old back roads that you know so well.'

'I like that plan, Hugh; although I think we had better lock the doors and windows of our motel rooms tightly and take it in turns to keep an eye out for prowlers tonight. These people might think that we've now seen a little too much, to be allowed out of the district so easily.'

'Well hopefully, after these planned phone calls, they'll think we're just a couple of amateurs who've been scared silly by tonight's events and just want to get back to our respective professions.' Hugh looked at his watch.

'Hmm. Past eight of the clock. I don't know about you, Miss Muffet, but I'm starting to feel a bit peckish. All this leaping off bridges and into wells seems to lend an edge to one's appetite.'

'Trust you to be thinking about food,' Tessa bantered. 'With a bit of luck, there might be a cafe open in Mirambeena, or perhaps a roadside diner out on the highway.'

Chapter Nine

IN THE EARLY HOURS of Sunday morning, Tessa and Hugh issued from their motel doors, loaded suitcases rather ostentatiously into their respective vehicles, and drove off in the darkness, much in the manner of two interstate travellers keen to make an early start. The occupant of a big Ford F100 utility truck, parked across from the motel but clearly visible under a street-light, seemed to be taking an inordinate interest in their activities, as did a furtive figure who darted in and out of a driveway next to a nearby auto-electrician's premises. If any further proof were needed that their movements were being closely scrutinised, it was amply supplied when they drove off, for a pair of headlights lanced from a laneway not far from the motel and the vehicle followed them in convoy out of town.

A glance in Hugh's rear view mirror suggested the outline of a large sedan, which revealed itself as a Ford Falcon when it abruptly pulled out and passed both the Land Rover and the Fiat at high speed. To Tessa in particular it bore all the hallmarks of an unmarked police car, its present deployment as an observation platform becoming obvious when it pulled off the road half a mile further on, only to swing back into formation behind them once they had cruised sedately past.

This cat and mouse game continued for some

distance along the winding road which climbed from Mirambeena toward the southern Darling Downs, until at last the driver of the Falcon appeared to be convinced that his quarries were indeed heading for the New England Highway *en route* to the New South Wales border. The Ford had been tail-gating the Land Rover as it laboured up a steep incline, but when a narrow side-track offered a convenient turning point halfway up the slope, the pursuer abruptly abandoned the chase, braking savagely and executing a gravel-spitting U-turn. Hugh was both relieved and delighted to find the glaring headlamps, which for miles had seared into his rear view mirror, suddenly replaced by rapidly receding tail-lights.

Tessa, who had been restraining the Fiat so as to stay just a few car lengths ahead of the Land Rover, was also pleased to note only one set of lights following, and made a Churchillian victory sign with a hand thrust outside her driver's window. A few miles further on, she indicated a left turn and a moment later, followed by Hugh, she was nosing the little car along a rutted dirt track which appeared to be nothing more than a laneway between isolated cattle paddocks. In this terrain, the Fiat was far less at home than the Land Rover and, mindful of the car's low ground clearance, Tessa had to keep her driver's side wheels up on the track's high centre hump, slowing to a crawl and inching her way around innumerable washouts and potholes. Hugh hung back at a discreet distance, marvelling at the girl's skill and sense of direction as she guided them up another side track, over a wooden grid and along what was clearly a private road through a lantana-infested grazing property. When at last they stopped at a barbed wire gate, Hugh jumped down from his vehicle and sprinted forward to open it.

'Allow me, Miss Muffet,' he said gallantly. 'I need to refresh my memory of these ingenious, yet so often recalcitrant, devices.' With a smile, she watched him in the headlights while he detached a wire loop from a wooden stake, un-twisted the stake from the top strand of the gate, lifted the gate's end-post clear of a retaining loop at the base of the fence, then swung the whole crazily sagging structure open. It wasn't every day that one saw a bush gate of that type opened by a man in checked shirt and knitted tie, waistcoat and Barbour jacket, with a flat tweed cap atop his head. But Hugh was a countryman to the core, she reflected, and his pastoral, neo-Romantic spirit somehow seemed just at much at home in the wide, brown spaces as it did in the softer-hued landscapes of his native isles. Like her, he was one of those rare creatures equally at home in two supposedly distinct worlds, constantly using one to strengthen, enrich and inform the other.

'Ah, the good old Aussie farm gate,' Hugh smiled as Tessa drove through. 'Ingenious, practical and nothing else like it in the world.' He darted back to the Land Rover, drove it through the gap, then re-closed the gate behind them. They were now once more on a public road – albeit a very narrow, badly eroded and tortuously graded affair – which wended its way back over hill and dale, into the southern regions of the greater Mirambeena Valley.

As they rejoined the bitumen road that ran between Mirambeena and the little village of Junction Ridge, a faint glow was cresting the eastern ridges, and the battlements of Cattle Mountain were just becoming visible, rearing up dramatically into the crepuscular dawn. They drove past the small cluster of buildings at Junction Ridge *sans* headlights and with engines throttled low to avoid attention, then veered right where the road forked just beyond the village.

The route they had taken ran along the floor of a narrow valley, or defile, carved between two high ridge saddles, and several times they crisscrossed a babbling, serpentine creek via low causeways. Cattle Mountain was now on their left, forming the pinnacle of this valley's eastern wall. In short order, they were again turning right, darting up a side-road and thence onto another rough track which climbed at a dizzying angle toward the western ridge tops. Up there lay their destination – a secluded block of cattle country, accessible only in good weather via a series of little-used right-of-ways running between other isolated properties. The owner, a businessman whom Tessa's father had saved from financial difficulties many years earlier, now lived in a distant city, but he retained the place both for its sentimental value and as an occasional escape hatch – a bush haven, far removed from work pressures, for himself and a small coterie of trusted friends. The Scott family had a standing invitation to use the old place whenever they wanted or needed it.

It was a tricky task manoeuvring that little Italian sports car up the hillside, along a trail with memories in every metre, but at last they came to a place where a secluded, scrub-covered ravine fell away at right angles to the track and Tessa nosed the Fiat off into it. With Hugh's help she pulled aside a jumble of brush, fallen branches and bendable saplings sufficient to allow the vehicle entry into a hollow beneath overhanging trees. The pair then quickly set about concealing the car by dragging the foliage back into place. Fifteen minutes later, they were satisfied with their handiwork: with dawn breaking, the Fiat's bright red paintwork appeared to be well hidden even from airborne stickybeaks, and Tessa now joined Hugh in the Land Rover for the final, cross-country leg of the trip.

The four wheel drive soon left behind anything that could be regarded as a track, slipping and dodging this way and that, around the tops of gullies and gorges, through narrow gaps between belts of thick scrub and open forest, until at last they saw it – the old bark hut which they had used as a base last year, while investigating sightings of a mysterious carnivore. The rustic building nestled on a little shelf above a grassy gully, sheltered on each side by lightly-timbered, sloping spurs. Dew steamed off its corrugated iron roof in the first soft rays of the morning sun, and its open front – for it was in reality little more than a three-sided lean-to – exuded, almost radiated, a sense of cosy invitation.

'Home!' The two wayfarers yawned and stretched, smiling as they voiced the word in unison.

Chapter Ten

'AH, GOOD OLD Cattle Mountain, eh?' Hugh Bainbridge, seated on a fallen log and gazing east toward the towering peak, raised a tin pannikin in salutation. 'I've often conjured up that prospect over the past year, you know: had it *flash upon that inward eye,* as the Lake poet says.'

'A different sort of dreaming spire, eh?' Tess suggested. 'Yes, the old place gets into your psyche a bit, doesn't it?'

The sky was now a delicate pastel blue, and the mid-morning sun was doing its best to dispel the chill of the persistent sneaky breezes that eddied in over the western ridges and down through the gullies. The chortle of kookaburras and the crack of a distant whipbird lent ambience to the tang of wood smoke and the fragrance of billy tea, as the investigators sat back to consider their position and plan their next moves. The hours after daybreak had been spent in packing their meagre provisions into the lean-to, concealing the Land Rover in a nearby pocket of scrub, and then doing a quick reconnaissance of the spurs and gullies within a two square kilometre radius; until at last, satisfied that they had the immediate environs of the lean-to, plus a fair chunk of the valley's south-western slopes, completely to themselves, Tessa and Hugh had settled back to enjoy a cuppa. The fact that the only tracks back into that part of the range were generally used only by cattle and wallabies added to their sense of comfortable seclusion, until the drone of an approaching aircraft suddenly sent them ducking inside the building.

'Surely they're not *that* well organised,' Tessa protested angrily. 'That they run to aeroplanes.'

'No, it's not coming this way,' Hugh decided. 'It's travelling north, well away from us.'

'You're right; and it's a fair-sized passenger plane by the look of it; probably flying from northern New South Wales to one of the Queensland regional cities.'

'Makes one think, doesn't it? If we could only obtain access to a light plane ourselves, then get up topsides and have a good dekko up all the gullies, hills and dales of the whole district, we'd have a fair shot at locating the hiding place of that hulking monstrosity, in short order.'

'Hmm; although they're bound to have it well-concealed. Still, we can do the next best thing, I suppose. We can climb Cattle Mountain, and sundry other peaks about the place, and use field glasses to peruse every nook and cranny within a reasonable distance. It will mean a lot of foot-slogging but at least we should be able to keep a low profile and, with a bit of luck, we'll be able to discover and observe any suspicious characters, or things, before they observe us. If, after a few days, we don't discover anything, we could possibly start to make some discreet enquiries; perhaps visit some old acquaintances, being very careful how we approach them, of course.'

'Indeed; discretion being the better part of valour and all that.' Hugh peered around the lean-to. 'Let's see now. We haven't much in the way of supplies or kit, though I dare say we'll make do.'

'Yes; that highway service station where we ate last night certainly didn't run to a huge grocery section, but the advantage of its location was that we wouldn't have attracted attention out there with our purchases – we might have been travellers bound for just about anywhere: in any event there was nothing open in town at that time of night and, as they say, beggars can't be choosers.' Tess was now unpacking a cardboard box of stores onto the rough-hewn bench that stood in the middle of their shelter. 'Here we are then: one packet of Bushells tea, condensed milk, powdered milk, sugar, some old-ish flour, one tin of baked beans, one of peas. A few local potatoes and onions; oranges and apples; oh, and one packet of orange slice biscuits.'

'One packet of Vita Brits,' Hugh added, joining in the unpacking. 'One half loaf of white bread, the last on the stand; oh, and butter to go with it. In here meanwhile,' – here the professor turned his attention to an old cupboard in the corner – 'the odd pot, pan and tin plates, which obviously stay from year to year. That looks like the whole provender; although we may be able to supplement our supplies with game, or fish from the creek. I see you brought your rod, Tess.'

'Yes. It may really come in handy, before we're finished here.' She glanced eastward and smiled softly. 'Well Hugh, I know it's a fair step to Cattle Mountain, and we've had a reasonable walk already this morning, but do you think that perhaps it's time to press onward, downward and upward?'

'No time like the present, Miss Muffet.' Hugh was packing a vacuum flask, filled with tea from the billy, into a haversack which he draped across one shoulder. From the slim case that had been sent from England by Westmead, the professor then withdrew a classic Rigby bolt-action rifle, and slung that on his opposite shoulder. 'Just in case we encounter any of your wild boars,' he said.

Tessa, clad in a parka, jeans and hiking boots, now shouldered her fishing rod and the pair set off at an ambling, cautious pace down into the valley and towards the opposing saddle. They stuck mostly to the scrubby gullies, eschewing the often easier paths down ridge spurs so as to avoid outlining themselves against the horizon. A clear exception to this rule had to be made when crossing the public road which served the scattered properties at the valley's southernmost end, but as this was a gravel track which carried only occasional traffic, it could be approached unseen through lantana thickets and other scrub which grew on each side.

Once across that hurdle, and the nearby creek, they were virtually at the base of Cattle Mountain, and by pushing up another scrub-clad gully they could ascend half-way to the peak before breaking cover.

One o'clock found them at the pinnacle, ensconced among a tangle of shrubs, small trees and rocks, scattered across a little plateau which extended no more than fifteen feet in any direction. At their backs sat one giant boulder, secured on a ledge just below the lip of the peak by a narrow neck of wind-blasted granite and a cluster of smaller stones around its base. Tessa and Hugh, gratefully drinking tea and eating baked bean sandwiches, turned to marvel at the great rock's apparent defiance of gravity.

'It looks as if wind and rain over centuries have coursed down the fissures in the rock and eroded its actual base,' Tessa suggested. 'There certainly doesn't seem to be a lot left to prop it up.'

'One day – if there happens to be a minor earth tremor perhaps – it will simply topple off,' Hugh said. 'I'd hate to be making my way up the mountainside at that particular moment. Another sandwich, Miss Muffet?'

'Yes please. This clambering about in cold weather does give one an appetite, doesn't it? Worth the climb though, just for the view.'

The prospect was certainly a spectacular and rugged one. Far below, in the valleys on either side, meandering creek beds glittered in the afternoon sun, snaking around and sometimes crossing the stony gravel roads which ran between isolated homesteads. There were occasional small pockets of cultivation, backed by scrub-clad foothills and forested spurs rearing back into the ranges; and between some of these were gullies and ravines which funnelled deep into the hillsides and finished who knew where. But a perusal with Tessa's binoculars, and a brass pirate spyglass which Hugh had insisted on bringing, revealed no sign whatsoever of diabolical steam trains, or anything else that seemed remotely suspicious.

After an hour or more spent in fruitless observation from this comfortable eyrie, the two amateur investigators prepared for the long walk back to base, with the idea of perhaps wetting a line in the creek *en route*.

'The least I can do is carry the haversack, Hugh,' Tessa insisted. 'Especially as it's much lighter now. You lugged it all the way up, after all – eh, what's that?'

The reason for the lawyer's consternation was at first hard to define: originating as something between a sound and a mere nerve-tingling sensation, it became the faintest tremble in the ground beneath their feet, steadily intensifying yet somehow remaining vague and distant, as if its motive force originated many miles away, deep in the earth's core.

'Surely that's not the earth tremor you were talking about before,' Tessa said worriedly, for as the shudder increased, a mild vibration seemed to seize the vast boulder beside them. They watched, fascinated, for a minute or more, until the disturbance eddied away and the huge rock regained its equilibrium.

'I say, this region isn't prone to seismic instability, is it?' Hugh wondered.

'Not that I'm aware of,' Tessa replied. 'First time for everything, I suppose.'

The shadows were deepening in the scrub as they trudged back down the mountainside gully, to arrive at last at the creek, and the mossy stepping stones they had used earlier in the day. A bend in the watercourse, sheltered by lantana thickets and trees which reached out from either bank to interlace above a glassy pool, provided a welcome rest area, a cosy nook all but invisible from the adjacent road. Diffused shafts of sunlight dappled the surface of the water, and glistening perch could be seen cruising through the pellucid stream as it coursed along its pebbled bed. A catfish shuffled over the muddy bottom of a limpid pool below the opposite bank, while a shape that may have been an eel was just visible beneath a blanket of moss further downstream.

It was an idyll worthy of Walton, and Tessa quickly responded to the challenge with her angling tackle, but as time wore on it seemed the fish were either too well-fed, too clever or they were simply bored by the flies on offer. An hour's futile casting made it patently obvious that baked beans would again be on the menu for the evening meal.

'Oh well, there's always tomorrow,' the girl said optimistically, packing up her rod. 'Some worms might do the trick. Hello, hello!'

The sound of a car engine nearby put them both on sudden alert, and from behind their screen of lantana they watched as an old Dodge utility splashed its way over the nearby causeway and trundled off down the road. The pen on the small truck's tray, and the noisy heifer within, suggested a farmer about his normal business, and the two investigators again took pause to wonder. Was this really a community in thrall to kidnappers, corrupt officialdom, or some monstrous infernal machine? On a placid afternoon like this, it was hard to conceive of such things, and yet the inescapable facts remained: Angie Reimann was missing; so were Warren Schultz, Jemima Blackman and a host of others. Only last night, a man claiming to be a policeman had physically attacked Tessa, and Hugh had been forced to leap off a railway bridge to escape something which for all the world resembled a vintage steam engine. There was something topsy-turvy about all this, and even the learned professor found himself groping for a satisfactory form of words to address it.

'We can't be imagining all this, Tess. After all,

that – that thing, which ran you off the road last night and chased me halfway across a field and down a well – well, it was hardly one of the Reverend Awdry's benevolent literary creations. It *was* material, surely. It's something which has been specifically designed and engineered by someone, and it's being used deliberately by certain parties, for some sort of skulduggery. And speaking personally, I'm dashed if I'll see a blackguard like that Arblaster get away with it!'

'Jolly well said, Hugh,' Tessa grinned. 'I'm with you. Homeward ho then, and let's discuss the subject over some sort of sustenance.'

THE WIND HAD dropped during the afternoon and the night was clear and cold. Tessa and Hugh, with blankets wrapped around their shoulders, huddled close to the fireplace, eating steaming mashed potato and baked beans on toast. From a nearby ridge, a chorus of dingoes lent an awe-inspiring, primeval accompaniment to their sense of splendid isolation.

'That old siren song,' Hugh said, picking up a tea cup. 'Our worthy ancestors, across the globe and down the millennia, must all have heard a similar chord progression. We're privileged to hear it still.'

'It binds us, doesn't it?' Tessa reflected. 'So many generations, linked by such a call. Something like that adds so much to our sense of continuity –

a constant, if you will, through times of relentless change. In a strange way though, it increases my concern for someone like Jem Blackman.'

'How so, Muffet?'

'Well, I'm speculating, of course, because we don't really know where she is. For all we know, she could be locked up in a safe house or a prison cell in the middle of town. But a sound like that, I'm sure, would unnerve her. She's not one for constancy, or the age-old things. For her, it's all innovation, and change, and the rational pursuit of efficiency.'

' She's an ardent utilitarian, I gather.'

'One hundred per cent, cast iron,' Tessa smiled. 'Her pet peeves are the humanities in the academic realm, any form of business regulation, public housing, public libraries – oh, and trade unions. She seems to dislike the latter with a special passion.'

'Hmm.' Hugh frowned. 'Well, as to the latter, we all know that they contain some extreme elements. Some of our chaps in Britain are certainly a bit beyond the pale. But there are some bad elements in the business sector, too, and the unions surely have a clear and vital role to play in any free society, as a check and balance on behalf of working people. As to public housing: well, I generally steer clear of politics, but my lot have been associated down the years with the Red Tory tradition – from Disraeli to Macmillan – and I tend to share their view that there's something manifestly wrong with any wealthy society that denies its families a secure hearth and home.'

'I agree wholeheartedly, Hugh,' Tessa said. 'But to Jemima's way of thinking, and a few others in her political circles these days, there exists a set of seemingly immutable, natural laws – to wit market forces – which rule out almost any form of active assistance to those less well off. These laws govern every transaction, totally, and they are apparently resistant to any form of human intervention or modification: there seems to be little room in this creed for active stewardship of the economy, and if people end up in trouble it is always entirely of their own making.'

'Well, of course, that harks back to Malthus and Ricardo and all those *laissez faire* purist chaps of the late eighteenth and early nineteenth centuries, doesn't it? Unfortunately it does seem to be rearing its ugly head again; even gathering a number of extreme adherents within the major political parties around the world. How does your *pater* view it?'

'With alarm. At heart, he's an interventionist in economic matters, and despite his conservative badging, he's always been for the underdog. Of course, he's in the junior coalition party: as to the major party – the Liberals – well, the Prime Minister is certainly no hard liner or radical monetarist, but there appears to be any number of people on the fringes, in think tanks and such like, who are pushing a fairly solid, right wing agenda, particularly those seeking to kick-start political careers. To them, welfare bashing and union baiting are clarion calls.'

'Like Jemima?' Hugh wondered. 'Do you know her well, Tess?'

'Not that well really. We were in a few classes together at university; her aim was never a legal degree of course, but she studied business law, and some related subjects. And we're both members of the university senate these days.' Tessa took a sip of tea from a scalding mug and for a moment appeared lost in thought. 'She's actually a very bright person to meet socially – not at all a dour old thing like some people imagine. She's vivacious and engaging, with a wacky sense of humour, but she also knows how to make herself very unpopular at times.'

'Been successful in business, I gather?'

'Very much so. A brilliant entrepreneur and market strategist. Which reminds me…' Tess broke off to snatch up a document from the nearby bench. 'This prospectus of Arblaster's – the one we postponed reading last night after all the action of the afternoon and early evening. I was having a peek just before dinner and it would appear that, amongst the many business interests in our friend's diverse portfolio, he is a major shareholder and an executive director of Western Colliery Holdings.'

'A coal mining company?' Hugh shot a surprised glance at Tessa. 'Well, that might explain where he sources the fuel for his infernal creation.'

'Perhaps'. Tessa wrinkled her nose as she put on a small pair of glasses, a practice which she found increasingly necessary for night reading, while Hugh focussed a meagre torch light on the prospectus. 'The only problem is that the company title is something of a misnomer, these days anyway. According to this – and one assumes it is a legal, public document – the actual collieries, located in the Ipswich and Mirambeena region, were worked out years ago. The company has since diversified into all sorts of seemingly unrelated areas – telecommunications, real estate, steel and aluminium; even brewing for goodness' sake. In short, they seem to have become something of a speculative investment group – takeover specialists, corporate raiders even.'

'Hmm. That sounds feasible – especially the takeover part.'

'Yes. But here's something else that's interesting. It says here that they have recently made an offer to shareholders of Bishop Industrial Gases, with the aim of gaining control of that company and thus enhancing returns for Western Colliery Shareholders, through acquisition of a highly profitable export earner.'

'And I seem to recall you telling me that Bishop

is Jemima Blackman's company.' Hugh whistled as he dunked an orange slice biscuit in his cup of tea.

'It certainly is,' Tessa confirmed. 'But that's where the prospectus appears to be out of date, because I remember reading in our firm's business report, a couple of months ago, that Jemima had outmanoeuvred the strategists behind a Queensland-based, hostile takeover bid, and had sent the would-be raiders packing.'

'Aha! A motive perchance,' cried Hugh. 'By thunder, it's not impossible. Your acquaintance stymies a takeover by friend Arblaster: he's not the chap to take 'no' for an answer, so his response is to kidnap poor old Jemima and force a business capitulation.'

'It certainly isn't beyond the realms of possibility, is it?' Tessa agreed. 'The more you think of it, the more credible it becomes. But why abduct all these other people? Most of them don't appear to be wealthy, or well-connected.'

'Just a ruse perhaps, to throw any investigation off the scent. With all sorts of people – tradesmen, farmers, teachers, etc – going missing, it makes it that much harder to establish a link to pure corporate rivalry as the major motive.'

'Yes; and having corrupt police in charge of the investigation makes it easier still to conceal one's tracks. But why such an elaborate scheme, with a giant locomotive running about? It's so preposterous. Why not simply sneak around in cars and quietly nab all the people they want – as they appear to have done in certain cases, notably Angela and her parents?'

Hugh shook his head. 'A magnificent obsession perhaps? According to that letter sent to James Wyatt, who was of course one of the original engineers who designed the *Diablo*, Arblaster has ideas of re-establishing steam as a major means of propulsion right across the world. And he actually intimated that, did he not, in the conversation he had with us? Of course, he also described the *Diablo* as an "antiquated, unstable monstrosity" when he spoke to me on the telephone.'

'Hmm. Another attempt to mislead, for sure.' Tessa stood up to stretch her legs, gazing out at the brilliant stellar formations in the cold, clear sky. 'Whatever its means of propulsion, that thing is hardly antiquated – or unstable.'

Hugh joined Tessa at the edge of the lean-to, where they stood for a moment side by side.

'*And at night the wondrous glory of the everlasting stars*,' he said quietly.

Tessa looked up into the professor's face, and smiled softly. 'Why Hugh; you're quoting the bush bards.'

'And why not, Miss Muffett?' he replied. 'Mr Paterson must be one of the most quotable, rollicking versifiers in the history of the language.'

Chapter Eleven

IT WAS HARD to get out of bed on Monday morning. The first faint rays of dawn glinted off icicles dangling from a nearby fence, while far below the gully bottoms and creek flats were carpeted in a shimmering frosty white. The most amazing thing for Tess and Hugh, observing from the snugness of their bunks, was the way the hillside itself awoke, as a myriad small, huddled shapes, dotted across the grassy slope below their shelter, suddenly began to stir. A peeping sun at length transformed these vague forms into wallabies, who slowly ambled off, crouching on all fours, to forage for the daintiest pickings that daylight could reveal.

'Remarkable sight, Tess,' Hugh suggested at length.

'It certainly is,' Tessa flicked back wisps of hair from her face and rubbed her hands. 'I suppose we should really be joining them at breakfast. Vita-Brits? Tea? Or perhaps just a little while longer in bed?'

'Brr! A little longer in bed, I think. There's a nip in the air worthy of late Michaelmas.'

The day's activities could not be shirked for long, however, and rekindling the waning fire became the first priority. It was difficult at first to coax droplets of water from the squat rainwater tank behind the lean-to, but a burning brand applied to the barrel of the frozen brass tap soon freed up the flow of liquid. Before long a fresh billy of tea, accompanied by bowls of breakfast biscuits soaked in hot water and condensed milk, was assisting the thawing process of the two hut dwellers. In under an hour they were again on the march, bypassing Cattle Mountain via a more northerly ridge crossing; then making for an even more distant peak – known to Tessa as the 'Jump-Up' – which would hopefully provide them with a bird's eye view into other valleys and creek beds, further to the east.

The aim of the investigators was to quarter as much of the southern Mirambeena district as possible, staying between two known *Diablo* sighting points – Cattle Mountain and Schaefer's Grove. The area was large and the terrain tough, but the prospect from the higher points of the ridges was considerable and it seemed likely that both the errant locomotive – and its captives if they were still safe and sound – would have to be hidden back in some of the region's more remote fastnesses, rather than in the more closely-settled country around Mirambeena and Layton. From the higher crests there was also the opportunity to unobtrusively observe the movements, however infrequent, of traffic and people along the back roads, with the possibility of gaining some insight into the true strength of Inspector Jensen's loudly-vaunted spy network.

By late afternoon, the weary travellers were forced to acknowledge that their second day of searching had once again yielded minimal results. The view from the peak of the Jump-Up, where they spent some two hours in the middle of the day, revealed only the quotidian reality of isolated farmhouses, a long-unpainted milking shed, an occasional farm truck or utility pursued along the byways by a rooster-tail of dust, and an old Ferguson tractor, ploughing one of the small pockets of cultivation etched on the narrow strips of flat land available between creek beds and mountain foothills.

Apart from the fact that Tessa bagged a much-needed duck for their dinner, their day-long rambles over some seventeen miles of countryside appeared to have done nothing to assist their investigation. The only other noteworthy event, which they noticed as they trudged home across the valley floor below Cattle Mountain, was another slight earth tremor, similar to, though milder than, that of the previous day.

'An aftershock from yesterday perhaps,' Tessa suggested. 'I've read that areas affected by a seismic disturbance will often experience a succession of minor tremors, following days apart.'

'Hmm. Well, at least we don't have to worry too much about crockery,' Hugh smiled.

The old hut was a welcome sight as they approached through the gathering dusk. 'Hearth and home,' the professor pronounced. 'I'm glad we stacked in some fire wood before we left.'

'Yes indeed. It's great that the old bush shower is still there too. Don't know about you, but I feel sweaty despite the cold weather.'

'I'll get some water on the boil,' Hugh said. 'Then while you're showering, I'll get some dinner organised.'

'Sounds marvellous.' Tessa checked her shotgun before sliding it back in its zippered case, and then sat down on a bunk to remove her boots. Hugh started a fire in the old wood stove, sat a saucepan of water on one of the hot plates, then surrounded the duck with some potatoes in a pan, which he slid into the oven. Tessa had cleaned the bird during a rest stop in a gully, well before they arrived home, and while she now showered under a rudimentary rope and bucket device behind the lean-to, Hugh set about demonstrating his culinary skills. He added to the pan some stinging nettles which Tessa had carefully collected from the creek bank, and arranged some bush cherries on two tin plates. He then kneaded some flour, butter and salt for damper and set the mixture to bake beside the pan. Bush showers being generally short-lived affairs, especially on a cold evening, Tessa was soon back inside the lean-to and took over basting the poultry and potatoes while Hugh cleaned up.

Two weary but contented travellers again partook of their evening meal next to the fire, gazing out at a brilliant panoply of stars which arched down from their lean-to roof toward the south-eastern ridges. The sky-scape was studded here and there by gum trees which shimmered ghostly in the moonlight, and once again a dingo howled to some companions on a distant ridge. Not too far away, a cow replied softly to the nervous murmur of its calf, their familiar domestic notes a faint reminder that other human habitation probably did still exist, somewhere within the known universe. They were drinking tea, with Tessa leaning back against Hugh's shoulder, before either felt the need to speak.

'It's wonderful to be back here, isn't it?' Tessa said at length, still gazing, slightly awe-struck, at the stars. 'On a night like this. And if circumstances were different, it would be the most marvellous holiday; the best ever, as we used to say when we went camping as kids. It's just that –.' Her voice trailed off as she turned her head and met Hugh's thoughtful gaze.

'I know what you mean, Muffet,' he said gently. 'Those good people are still missing, and we don't appear to have discovered any real clues to their whereabouts as yet. We've not seen hide nor hair of this jolly locomotive either.'

'At least we appear to have avoided detection so far. With a bit of luck, the opposition thinks we are somewhere in regional New South Wales, instead of in their backyard.'

'Quite. And even an occasional shot, like yours this afternoon, should go unremarked, out in the bush.'

'Yes; it's not at all unusual, at this time of year, for hunters to be out and about; after duck, or hare, or something else for the pot. And you'll often hear a farmer having a go at foxes or wild pigs. I suppose though that we are going to have to take the bit between the teeth before much longer, and start approaching some of the locals for information. Another day or so, perhaps, of independent searching and, if we're still none the wiser, I vote we pay a discreet yet casual visit to some of the local farming fraternity. We don't have to act as if we're on some grand investigation: people will often volunteer information, if they feel something unusual is going on.'

'That certainly seems the most logical step now,' Hugh agreed. 'People in the countryside notice things – different faces; strange vehicles poking about; unusual activities or strange behaviour on the part of neighbours. And they're often willing to share – I say! What's that light? It seems to be coming straight up the jolly mountain, along one of the ridge spurs. A spotlight?'

'Too powerful surely. The beam is like a lighthouse beacon; and you're right, it's not being generated down on the valley floor: whatever vehicle is behind the light is actually climbing the lower foothills. Surely they haven't twigged to us, and sent the confounded train up into the mountains on our trail? Or *has* the damned thing got a mind of its own, and it's actively seeking us out?'

'The mind boggles.' Hugh picked up his telescope and walked to the edge of the lean-to, watching as the light ascended above the scrub line, then abruptly changed direction, travelling almost horizontal to their position across the ridge spurs, through open forest country. Tessa grabbed her binoculars and joined the professor at the front of the shelter, where the pair stood for a moment as if spellbound, their glasses boosting to realistic proportions what had looked at first like a fiery toy locomotive, towing a trio of lighted Tonka carriages. As the *Diablo* crossed perhaps half a mile below, they could make out strange, grotesquely-melting shapes and shadows, darting and flickering about in the wan glow inside the cars; while a vast swelling drone, punctuated by the throb and clank of moving metal, drifted up the hillside, drowning and stilling the nocturnal sounds and movements of bush and paddock.

'*And instead of lowing cattle, I can hear the fiendish rattle*,' Hugh murmured, when at last the blazing apparition dissolved into the gullies and ridges to the north-east, and the mountainside had once more lapsed into a welcome silence. 'The game's afoot, Miss Muffet! We're on the right track, and no pun intended. It's here, headquartered somewhere not too far away.'

His eyes held a steely glitter as they turned back toward Tess.

'And I think that pretty well determines our direction first thing tomorrow,' the lawyer said. 'The course that train was on would take it into, and through, a couple of adjoining back country properties, not far from the actual homesteads. And one of those homesteads we know very well.'

'The Steiler brothers.'

'The same,' Tessa nodded, then made a wry grimace. 'Well, I hate to bring up something as prosaic as laundry, but I suppose there is still hot water on the stove and one must be practical.'

'From the thought springs the deed,' the professor suggested, tossing two days worth of dirty clothing into an old concrete tub next to the tankstand and flourishing a bar of soap.

But the evening's excitement was not yet over: as they finished their laundry and hung the wet clothes out in the cold night air to await tomorrow's sun, a piercing whistle rent the stillness, startling kookaburras into an uncharacteristic midnight chuckle and sending water-hens shrieking across a dam cradled in one of the nearby hollows. The *Diablo*, it seemed, was making a return journey, albeit on a different course. The unmistakeable sounds of its progress told that it was heading back to the valley floor, but this time it was plunging down one of the cleared gullies north of the investigators' camp, denying them a second side-on view. All told, it had been an exhausting day. The lean-to bunks beckoned, and sleep had become a priority that banished further talk or contemplation – until suddenly, from far off in the plutonic depths, another faint earth tremor came shivering up the spur and throbbing across the mountainside.

'More aftershocks?' Tessa wondered. 'Or something to do with that diabolical train?'

'A question for the new day, I think.' Hugh grinned and yawned luxuriously. 'I'm beat.'

Chapter Twelve
Tuesday 19th July 7.45am

IN A FLAT CLEARING surrounded on three sides by scrub-covered slopes, a small, unpainted weatherboard cottage sat expectantly, smoke billowing from its chimney toward the wan morning sky. Toward it, with the unhurried yet purposeful gait of the bushman, a figure was striding – a lean, hard-muscled individual wearing a lumberjack's cap, with flaps folded down over the ears, an old windcheater covering a flannelette shirt that tucked into faded blue jeans, and elastic-sided boots which crunched on the icy grass of the track. In one hand was an ancient Lithgow single-shot .22 rifle; in the other a large, recently-bagged scrub turkey.

Periodically the man glanced over his shoulder and though he approached the house at an even pace, there was an occasional look of extreme wariness, close to fear, on his open, candid face. He was almost at the front steps when a crisp voice from the nearby scrub made him spin around in utter amazement.

'Walter Steiler! Well met, sir!' As the words echoed across the clearing, a tall, dapper figure in a tweed jacket and flat cap emerged from the undergrowth.

'Frig me roan horse!' the bushman roared. 'Emil, it's the professor. Emil! You in there? Get outa bed, you lazy bugger, and get the kettle on. We got a visitor.'

The door creaked open and onto the porch ambled a figure a little stouter than, but otherwise strikingly similar to, the one bellowing on the track outside. 'Well, I'll be buggered,' proclaimed Emil Steiler, after an appraising pause and a shake of his greying curly locks. 'It *is* the professor. Well, he said he'd be back.'

'So did I,' a cheery female voice called from nearby. The two bushmen shifted their gaze toward Tessa Scott, her up-turned parka hood framing a beaming smile as she emerged from the scrub.

'And the lawyer's here too,' yelled Walter Steiler. 'Emil, watch your bloody language. There's a lady present. I hope you've got that house tidy, man.'

'Aw, Tessa's not too 'ouse-proud,' replied Emil, starting down the steps. 'She told us that last time.'

'No, I'm not,' Tessa said, walking forward to give both the unshaven men a hug and a kiss on the cheek. 'As long as that kettle's on, I'll forgive anything.'

'Good to see ya, Tessa.' Walter and Emil, both grinning like lottery winners, now turned toward the professor. 'How ya goin', Hugh?' The brothers spoke virtually in unison, shaking hands vigorously as Bainbridge greeted each in turn.

'Wally; Emil. It's darn good to see you chaps. How's the world been treating you?'

'Aw, not bad, not bad.' Walter, the elder and more voluble of the two brothers, handed his rifle, bolt-open and chamber empty, up to his brother. 'Seasons have been pretty good, ya know. Good rain a few weeks back; put a good fresh in the creek. Been some bloody funny things goin' on around here just lately though. I'll tell you about it inside over a cuppa, eh? Just give us a few minutes while I pluck this turkey and put him in some vinegar water to soak. By that time, Emil should have the kettle boiled and a pot o' tea on the go.'

'Need a hand, Wally?' Tessa offered.

'Na, Tess. Go in and make yourself comfortable, luv. You pair have probably walked a fair distance since sun-up. Go in and take the load off yer feet. Emil'll look after yer guns – just stick 'em in the corner with ours, anyway.'

'So you've still got the Rigby, Hugh?' Emil observed, as the professor placed the .275 in a cupboard alongside the Steiler brothers' small battery.

'Oh yes, Emil. Well, it's almost a family heirloom, really.'

'Could I just try the swing on your Browning, Tess?' Emil wondered. 'That's a good-lookin' gun – and such good balance too. They reckon they got better balance than the 5 shot, eh?'

' Well, Dad's got a 5 shot and he likes it,' Tess said. 'But I prefer the 2. I shoot clay targets with it a fair bit and I reckon it's as well-balanced as most of the under and overs that I've tried – less recoil too. Mind you, I bet Hugh will say that the Cashmore side by side is better than any of them.' She winked at the professor.

'Indeed I would,' Hugh confirmed with a laugh.

'Well, he's gotta say that, luv. He is an Englishman, you know.' Continuing the banter, Emil busied himself with kettle, teapot and cups, while his visitors' gaze travelled up and around the walls, drinking in an array of exquisitely carved plates and wall plaques which the Steilers had over the years fashioned from fallen scrub timber. It was traditional craftsmanship of a style becoming rare, which had garnered the bushmen dozens of prizes in agricultural shows, yet interest shown by guests in the work was always lightly dismissed.

'Yeah – couple o' new ones up there, eh?' Emil drawled. 'Prob'ly be better used as kindlin'.'

'No way,' said Tessa. 'I know art shops in Sydney whose proprietors would love to get their hands on them.'

'Oh, we just slap 'em up.' Emil placed a tray of chunky buttered toast and a steaming brew on the wooden kitchen table. 'Fills in a bit o' time.'

'Is he lookin' after yous, then?' Walter enquired, as he strolled in, scrubbed his hands at the sink and then shot an appraising glance at the table. 'Looks as if he has put on a decent spread, after all. You've done all right, fella, for once in your bloody life.'

'He certainly has,' Tess said, biting into some

toast with alacrity. 'And I'm famished enough to do it full justice.'

'Jolly good show this,' Hugh agreed. 'Fall to, then, and don't spare the waistlines.'

'Well, I don't reckon either of you two blokes has got to worry too much about waistlines,' adjudged Walter, pouring himself some tea. 'This is home-made bread, you know. Made it myself last night, and it's not half bad, is it? Well, I was gonna tell ya about some o' the funny bloody things goin' on around the place lately, wasn't I?'

The visitors nodded eagerly, and Wally was quick to continue. 'So, I s'pose you've both heard about all this ghost train business – people disappearin' around the valley and what have you?'

'Well, as a matter of fact, Wally, that's what brought us here this trip,' Tessa confided.

'I knew it,' Walter grinned hugely. 'I said to meself when I first saw you blokes: I said, that Tessa, she can't resist a mystery; and that Hugh's no different. I reckoned, soon as I saw you, that you'd be here about that train. I'll tell you what though, this bloody *choo choo* business has gone past a joke, now.'

'How so, Wally?' Hugh enquired.

'Well, o' course, at the start, we were takin' the whole thing with a pinch o' salt – that's at the start! What with all the newspaper and TV reports, people blowin' into town and makin' up stories about a "phantom express" and what not, it all sounded a bit far-fetched. "Pull the other one", we both reckoned. But then a couple o' weeks ago, we started hearin' things up here ourselves. Sounded like a bloody train whistle in the middle o' the night. I said to Emil – 'cause we both heard it – I said, the nearest train line's fifteen, maybe twenty miles away. Even on the clearest, stillest night, we've never heard a train before. And then o' course, there's the business with Ronny, the next door neighbour. You remember Ronny Weiss – lives just across the hill, in the next gully?'

'Yes,' Tess recalled. 'With the jumping cattle dog?'

'Yeah – clever bugger, eh, that dog? Can jump clean off the ground onto the top of a fence post. Well, the other afternoon, ol' Ronny comes roarin' in here in his ol' Mainline ute. He'd been out in the paddock, he reckoned, lookin' at fences, when all of a sudden, a train goes past – straight through the top o' his place. "I seen it," he yells at the top of his voice – he was worked up so much he was fairly screechin' at Emil and me – "I've seen the bloody ghost train, runnin' through the paddock without any tracks."

' "Whoa, whoa; settle down, Ronny," I says to him. "You must have been dreamin', mate – a train can't go where there's no bloody tracks."

' "I seen it, I tell ya," he says. "Broad flamin' daylight, and only about six or seven chain away. I know what I bloody saw."

' "All right, all right," we say. "Keep your shirt on. If you reckon you saw it, you prob'ly saw it. What do you want to do about it?"

'Well, he reckoned he was gonna go and see the p'lice in Mirambeena. We told him to ring 'em up on our phone – Ronny and his missus have never had the phone put on, you know – so he did that, but he got a bit put off because they didn't seem to be takin' him too seriously.'

Tessa and Hugh exchanged knowing glances, while Emil shoved the toast tray toward them and Wally warmed further to his tale.

'Apparently the coppers said they might come out and have a look around the followin' mornin' but by late afternoon, they hadn't come, so Ronny comes over here again, rings up the copshop and revs it fair up 'em. The day after that, I was up the paddock on the horse, and I seen ol' Ronny through the fence – and he's callin' the coppers for everything under the sun.

' "Useless mob o' bastards," he reckons. "I'm gonna ring 'em up again and tell 'em that I'll get on to the commissioner, or the local member, or some bugger like that." Well, I says to him then, "look, why don't you just let it go, mate? – you know, you might have been mistaken." "Mistaken?" he says "- mistaken, my ar…!" – whoops – sorry, Tess – I'm getting' a bit carried away with me language.'

'It's fine, Wally,' Tessa smiled, leaning forward

encouragingly. 'Tell us; what happened then?'

'Well, I keep sayin' to him: "look, Ronny, there's no fences broken, an' no tracks – how *could* a train travel cross-country, in open forest, without metal tracks?" Then he shoves this under me nose.' Wally paused again to retrieve a glass jar from a nearby shelf, spilling the grimy black contents onto the table.

'Coal!' declared Hugh.

'Has to be, eh?' Wally looked at both guests for confirmation. 'Ol' Ronny picked it up in his paddock, just near where he saw the train.'

'And there are no coal seams for miles,' Tessa observed.

Wally nodded. 'Nearest'd be Rinehart's Ridge, I reckon, and that'd be bloody near thirty mile away.'

'So what happened next, Wally?' Hugh prompted.

'Well, ol' Ronny rings the coppers up again, an' fairly blows the socks off 'em. Gets talkin' to an Inspector Jensen apparently, who's s'posed to be in charge o' the whole investigation into the train business. This Jensen tells him they're on top o' the whole thing – followin' up leads and what not – but they want to keep everythin' low-key, otherwise it could alert certain people, or cause a panic. He tells Ronny that if he sees or hears the train again, he should try an' get up close and get a good description. Well, I said to Ronny, "I dunno about that part of it, mate. It might be askin' for trouble to get too close. You dunno what that thing's capable of." Well, Ronny couldn't care less; he says to me, "I reckon I'll have a go, mate. Next time I go out in the paddock, I'll pick up a flamin' big waddy, or take a gun with me. The bloody thing won't get me in a hurry." Trouble is, it looks as if it might have.'

'You don't say so? Your neighbour's gone missing now?' Hugh looked askance at Tessa, while Wally Steiler drew breath and drank some tea.

'Yeah, well, we can't be sure what's happened yet, I s'pose. Sunday afternoon, just after lunch, we thought we heard a train again, and apparently ol' Ronny had gone up the paddock. Well, he never come back it seems. Peg – that's Ronny's better 'alf – walked all the way over here to tell us and ring the cops. We looked all round the paddock and saw no sign of him. Then late in the afternoon the cops showed up at Ronny's place and told us all to go home – they'd be bringin' in people – special investigators they said – and the place was now a crime scene and off limits. After that, Peg went off to stay with relatives in Toowoomba and we haven't heard from her since late Sunday arvo. I went out lookin' for a turkey this mornin' – managed to get one over in the scrub gully just after daylight – and I looked over into Weiss's place as I went by. Didn't see anythin' over there, but I don't mind tellin' ya, I was lookin' over me shoulder all the way out and all the way home. What with everythin' goin' on over the last few days and then last night's episode, it's enough to make any bugger nervous, I reckon. When I saw you blokes here now I was pretty relieved actually – thought it'd be good to get someone else's ideas on the whole business.'

'This episode last night, Wally?' Tessa wondered. 'What happened? Something unusual here at your place?'

'My oath. Wait'll you hear this one. You know, as I was sayin' before, Emil and I found it hard to believe this train business at first, although we were startin' to change our minds after hearin' whistles and all sorts o' sounds off in the distance. Then o' course Ronny seemed to be so convinced that he'd seen it, and he showed us the coal that he found. Then he went missin' – I s'pose there could be some other reason for that, but it's hard to see him fallin' into a gully and neither us nor the cops findin' him. What with all the weight of evidence, as you might say, we were pretty much converted to believin' in the thing – but last night was the clincher. About ten o'clock, it would have been, we heard all the sounds of a train – you know: bells, whistles, steam hissin', wheels clankin' and what have you. We run outside, and we could just make out a light movin' across the ridge, 'bout half-way up. It was above the scrub line, in the open forest, but from the angle we were lookin' from, the scrub stopped us from gettin' a clear view. Within a minute or so, the light disappeared over into Ronny's gully.'

'Did you see or hear it come back?' Hugh asked.

'Yeah, mate. 'Bout half an hour later, we heard the bugger comin' back again on the return journey. This time I took the old 'scope I used to have on the .30/30 – that scope got damaged once and the crosshairs were buggered, but that rifle don't need one anyhow – still, it's a good spottin' scope, an' I managed to get a bit of a glimpse of the train before it went over into the next gully. I only saw th' arse end of it really, but it had one o' those roofed-in platforms at the back, like the ol' time train carriages used ter have, an' there looked to be a bloke standin' on it.' Wally paused, as if trying to recall details. 'I couldn't be a hundred percent certain if it was a person, really, just a weird shape movin' around. Damned if I know what to think about the whole thing.'

'So what do ya reckon?' asked Emil softly. 'Are we all goin' mad out here, or what?'

'Not at all,' said Tessa. 'We saw it too, from the lean-to.'

'Well I'll be buggered,' Wally sat back, shaking his head. 'So what do you blokes reckon we should do next? Get onto the cops again, I s'pose, and tell 'em what we saw last night?'

'Normally I'd be all for that approach,' Tessa said. 'But as long as this Inspector Jensen is in charge, it's probably useless. In fact, based on recent patterns, it might be an open invitation for the train to pay you a closer visit.'

'Fair dinkum?' Wally leaned forward again. 'You reckon he's in on it, whatever's goin' on?'

'Almost certainly,' said Hugh. 'Of course, proving his involvement may be a problem.'

'It's also difficult to know how far the corruption extends,' Tessa added. 'It could be a proper minefield working out who's in on the secret, and who isn't – and how many spies they have around the place. That's why we're staying back at the hut at the moment, until we get a bit of an idea what's going on.'

The Steiler brothers looked at one another in amazement, until at last Emil broke the silence. 'Who woulda thought, eh? I mean, you hear about these bad apples in the p'lice force, but you don't expect to come across 'em. An' what the heck does all this train business mean – what are they doin' with people?'

'Have you noticed any new faces around the district lately?' Tessa wondered. 'Any unusual activities, or behaviour?'

'Well, since last year, when you two was last up this way, we 'ave had one new neighbour move into the district,' Wally replied after a moment's thought. 'They bought Muller's old place – the story went 'round that they were gonna do up th' old dairy and convert it into holiday cabins. Funny part is, no one in the valley seems to have met 'em – they don't seem to live on the place at all, and they soon stuck up a lot o' signs sayin' *no trespassin*. A few tradesmen's trucks went up there, but the place still looks the same from th' outside – hasn't been painted or anythin'.'

'Is that the milking shed we saw from the peak yesterday?' Hugh asked.

'Yes,' the lawyer replied. 'Down on the East Hatton road, the other side of Cattle Mountain.'

'Interesting, what?' Hugh looked thoughtful. 'I don' t suppose either of you has noticed any earth tremors recently – any sort of ground movement?'

The brothers exchanged sidelong glances. 'Yeah, quite a few as a matter of fact,' Emil said. 'We were just talkin' about it th' other day. Nothin' like you'd imagine an earthquake to be, but just – well, shimmies – sorta like vibrations – comin' from deep down, or way off.'

'Ha, I wonder!' said Hugh eagerly. 'Do you have a map of the district, by any chance?'

'Yeah; got an RACQ one in here somewhere.' Wally was already rummaging in a sideboard cupboard. 'We don't use it much, mind you, but occasionally you get some poor bugger who gets lost and strays up here, and we can show 'em how to get home with this.' He unfolded the map on the kitchen table.

'Do you mind if I draw on it?' Hugh asked, brandishing a fountain pen.

'Go for your life, mate,' was the reply.

'Righto! What price this scenario? – coal mines here, on the eastern side of the Mirambeena Valley -' making a cross on the map next to Rinehart's Ridge, Hugh's pen nib now raced south-westward to a point just below Junction Ridge, bypassing the townships of Mirambeena and Layton, but intersecting *en route* with landmarks such as Schaefer's Grove, the Jump-Up and finally Cattle Mountain – 'old, worked-out coal mines with long abandoned mine shafts, perhaps leading into an underground tunnel, or network of same. That might explain the recent seismic phenomena, as the *Diablo* moves about below the surface – one wouldn't hear the distinct sound of a train but merely a rumble or mild vibration, much like one experiences on a city street, above an underground commuter system. This scenario could also explain how the confounded thing can appear, and disappear, in far-flung corners of the district, without being seen too often in transit.'

'By hell, it's no wonder he's a bloody professor.' Wally thumped the table in delight.

'He does have his moments,' agreed Tessa, shooting Hugh a winning smile.

'Now, I would imagine,' said Hugh, making another X mark beside his 'tunnel' line, 'that Muller's old dairy would be somewhere about here.'

'You got a good sense of direction, Hugh,' Wally congratulated. 'That's almost exactly where it'd be.

Must be all that time you spend up in the Scottish highlands, eh?'

'Beginner's luck, I think,' Hugh said, still bending to study the map. 'Or perhaps a smidgin of the gillies' tuition has finally sunk in.'

'You're far too modest, Hugh,' Tessa said, leaning on his shoulder and pointing a long index finger at the most recent mark on the paper. 'That milking shed of Muller's – you're thinking it might have been made into a prison of sorts, aren't you?'

Their eyes met. 'Might be worth a closer look,' Hugh suggested.

'Those milkin' bales are set well back in off the road,' Emil advised. 'And you could be seen a mile off if you were comin' in from the front. Might be better to approach it from the back – sneak in cross-country, across Cattle Mountain, then down through the scrub behind Muller's old place, and take a quiet gander.'

'So you chaps are willing to throw in your lot with a couple of desperados, then?' Hugh wondered.

'Try and bloody keep us away,' said Wally with a laugh. 'We can't have this sorta thing goin' on around the valley.'

Chapter Thirteen
Tuesday 19th July 3.10pm

IT WAS A SOFT mellow afternoon and the open forest country high up on the south-eastern slopes of Cattle Mountain was a mottled tapestry of green, brown and sandy gold. Some miles further to the east, the narrow pinnacle of the Jump-Up reared above a line of smaller hills, while closer in the foreground, the white ribbon of the East Hatton road and the grey outline of a rocky creek bed snaked and intertwined across the valley floor.

'We're just comin' up to the back o' Muller's old place now,' Wally Steiler said softly, pointing out some taut strands of barbed wire just ahead. 'That's their old fence line.'

'It's been kept in good order,' Tessa observed, testing the tension of the wire and preparing to get through. 'Now, fellas – I suppose this is where we split up?'

The foursome had been travelling in a reasonably relaxed and open fashion since mid-morning, walking cross-country from the Steiler brothers' farm. Had they encountered anyone, their guise was that of a mixed party of hunters – two shotgunners seeking quail and two riflemen looking for wild pig; now, however, that they were entering the outlying paddocks of a suspicious property, their pre-discussed plan was to divide forces and to reconnoitre cautiously, proceeding via two scrubby gullies, or ravines, which ran down between mountain spurs to the creek flats where the old Muller dairy stood. The tops of the gullies were about half a kilometre apart, so after negotiating the wire fence and deciding on a rendezvous point in a scrub-clad glade just behind the dairy, Hugh and Emil headed left while Tessa and Wally marched off to the south.

The floor of the more northerly gully was largely clear of undergrowth and vines, allowing Hugh and Emil to move easily and rapidly between thick stands of trees and shrubbery. Pausing only to consume some fruit, they kept any conversation low and brief, occasionally diverting from their path to climb the ravine walls and inspect the surrounding countryside. Most of the time, their descent was steady and uneventful, yet an inescapable tension somehow pervaded the atmosphere – a constant, nape-tingling sensation of entering enemy territory, of being watched.

WHOOSH! Suddenly the gully exploded in a cacophony of grunts, squeals and snapping branches, as a sow and litter of piglets burst noisily from cover, less than a dozen yards ahead. Emil, in the lead, snapped shut the breech of his old Iver Johnson single-barrel twelve gauge; a second later, he broke it open and turned with a sheepish grin to Hugh. 'Frightened buggery outa me,' he said softly. 'This flamin' train's got a man on edge, I reckon.'

'It certainly gave me a start,' Hugh concurred. 'Thankfully, she went in the right direction – away from us.'

OVER IN THE other gully meanwhile, Tessa and Wally were finding the downhill journey neither easy nor swift.

'Bloody wall o' lantana up ahead, luv,' the bushman proclaimed, wiping sweat from his brow and unslinging his haversack. 'I can't believe how overgrown it's got since the last time I was over here. Mind you, that was five or six years ago. Well, we could try slashin' through it with the cane knife, I s'pose, but that's gonna be noisy, and bloody hard work.' He unbuckled the khaki bag and withdrew a sheathed machette, the handle of which had protruded from the loose flap, then extracted two oranges and handed one to Tessa. 'That'll quench your thirst, luv,' he advised.

The lawyer needed little encouragement. 'Mmm – life saver,' she said, peeling the top off the fruit and sucking it gratefully. 'Now, I'm wondering if it would be easier just to climb out onto the spur and make our way down. Admittedly, we'd be more exposed to public view, but at least we could move quickly and quietly outside the scrub. Alternatively, is there perhaps another gully that we could travel down?'

Wally looked thoughtful. 'There is, further

south,' he said at length. 'But it's a fair distance to backtrack and get over into it. Beyond the spur next to us is a big hollow or depression, if I remember right, with very steep walls – almost cliffs – and there are two really steep gorges that drain out of it. It's all rugged and dangerous stuff, and it takes us further away from the dairy. On the other hand, the mouth of this gully, and the one Hugh and Emil are in, both feed into the same patch o' scrub, which runs nearly to the back o' the old dairy.'

'Perhaps we could walk down the spur for a little way and try cutting back into this gully further down,' Tessa suggested. 'With a bit of luck, the lantana might not be as thick closer to the flat. Mind you, that might be a silly suggestion because I don't know the south-eastern slopes of the mountain very well – most of my expeditions were on the western side, with occasional forays across the ridge onto the north-east slopes. We had ongoing permission to access the properties on both sides up there, but we never knew the Mullers very well.'

'Well, they kept to 'emselves a lot, although they never had any *no trespassin'* signs like this lot have; but that's a good idea, luv, to push outa this scrub and wander down the spur for a bit; let's try that.'

So saying, Wally shouldered his haversack, picked up his bolt-actioned .250/3000 Savage, and began the climb up the side of the gully, forcing aside vines to make Tessa's ascent easier. They were almost out into the open when a sudden flurry of movement and sound eddying up the spur made them both drop down flat in the undergrowth.

The vision which promptly materialised below their hiding place was astonishing; so utterly incongruous that Wally and Tessa paused to exchange quizzical sidelong glances, as a sort of mute confirmation that both had actually witnessed the same phenomenon. A young woman, dressed as if she were on her way to lunch at an exclusive metropolitan restaurant, was running up the mountainside. The lapels of her tailored jacket were askew, and a button of her exquisite print blouse was undone – hardly surprising considering the furious backward glances she kept flinging over her shoulder – but her mane of blonde hair valiantly held its coiffure, her dark trousers somehow maintained their elegant crease and her shoes (flat-heeled but with gold buckles no less) revealed only the merest hint of dust and minor scuffing.

Tessa shook her head in unfeigned admiration: say what you would about Jemima Blackman, she had to be the epitome of style and glamour under pressure. Somehow, some way, the business woman had clearly contrived both to keep up appearances *and* to escape her captors – and the latter very recently by the look of things, for it was obvious by her demeanour that she was running for her life and in fear of pursuit.

Clearly there was no time to lose. Tessa handed her shotgun to Wally, asked him to keep an eye out, threw a cautious look down the cattle pad which ran up the spur and then broke cover behind Ms Blackman, who had already flown past their position and was now a good twenty metres further up the slope.

'Jem! Jemima!' the lawyer called out. 'Jemima Blackman! Hold up a second.'

The blonde woman stopped, turning slowly around on the track, a sequence of emotions flickering across her expressive face like projections on a screen – that first confusion of seeing a familiar face in an unfamiliar setting; the shock of definite recognition; and finally an almost beatific look of relief and gratitude. 'Tessa! Tessa Scott,' she said, all doubts now banished by a beaming smile as she started back toward her rescuer. 'Well, I'll be. Fancy meeting you here.'

Tessa shot another glance back down the track. No pursuers were in view as yet, but it was apparent from Jemima's now rigid stare in that direction that one or more could soon be expected.

'Are you alright, Jemima?' Tessa's voice held an urgent note. 'We'd better get behind some cover – down in the gully here. It's a bit rough but we should be able to elude whoever's chasing you. Quickly; we'd better hurry.' Once more Tess turned her gaze downhill, to ensure before plunging into the scrub that her planned escape route was not even now being observed. Jemima's voice behind her was suddenly infused with a brittle, nervous laugh.

'I don't really think that's necessary, Tessa!'

The lawyer spun around, and to her utter amazement found herself staring into the barrel of a snub-nosed pistol.

'Poor old Tessa,' Jemima chuckled, the tiny gun poised between perfectly manicured fingers. 'Can't resist racing to the rescue: the original do-gooder and nosey parker. I must admit I found it very hard to believe when they told me you'd gone home. I always thought you'd stick around – that you'd still be somewhere in the district – but I never expected you to come walking into our clutches quite so easily.'

'You bitch!' Tessa said evenly, though her mind was racing. 'So: I gather your "disappearance" was in fact an elaborate hoax and far from fighting off a hostile takeover by Maurice Arblaster, as the financial press believe, you've gone into partnership with him.'

'I'd say more of a loose coalition than a partnership,' Ms Blackman corrected. 'A mutually beneficial arrangement, based on certain shared objectives. A joint venture, you might say, between North Shore *tres chic* and white shoe brigade.' Again you had to hand it to old Jemima: she had a ready wit and a nice line in wry humour – although for Tessa there were clearly more pressing matters to discuss.

'What have you done with Angela Reimann?' the lawyer demanded. 'And her parents? And Warren Schultz, and all those others? What gives you the right – you and your "joint venturers" – to roam around kidnapping people?'

'Dear me!' said Jemima. 'Aren't we on our high horse? All the offended *noblesse oblige* of the squattocracy on show. Well, perhaps you'd like to join them, and see how they're all getting on?' She motioned with her pistol barrel. 'That way, back down the hill.'

Tessa turned on her heel and started to walk back down the cattle pad. With Jemima and her gun just a few paces behind, and now an armed man panting up the hill to meet them, she dared not risk a sidelong glance toward Wally, who continued to lay low and still in the undergrowth. For his part, the bushman was almost beside himself, primarily with concern for Tessa's safety, but also with sheer anger at this sudden, totally unexpected turn of events. Silently he cursed in frustration at the sheer impossibility of taking any action, and waited.

Jemima, meanwhile, was quick to vent her feelings at the latest arrival on the scene. 'Where have you been, you fool?' she snapped. 'I could have run faster with a cast on one leg?'

'I – I'm prob'ly not as fit as you,' the man

puffed, embarrassment and exertion combining to produce a complexion of fiery red.

'Well, that's stating the obvious,' the blonde woman sneered derisively. 'A simple reconnaissance run up the hill, and you can't keep up. I hope the rest of the troops are in better condition than you. Surely, even if we are out in the middle of bloody nowhere, it's not too much to expect that we maintain a basic fitness regime. See that it's instituted tomorrow, Herman, for all the troops, guards and anyone who supervises in the compound.'

Troops! Figure of speech though it probably was, the word nonetheless sent a shudder down Tessa's spine, and continued to vex her imagination as she walked along. *Compound*? Just what were this lot playing at? Was it some sort of nutty militia? Or delusions of grandeur on a larger scale? Unfortunately, Jemima was not one of those movie megalomaniacs with an uncontrollable urge to instantly reveal all her ambitions to her prisoners: instead she pursued her own bantering and increasingly puerile manner of interrogation while they marched.

'So where's the learned professor then, Tessa? Now don't try and kid us that he's headed off to Sydney, darling, because I'm willing to bet that he's still holed up somewhere in the district, too. You know, when I first heard about him and looked him up in *Who's Who*, I thought he might be a bit old for you; but I can see the attraction now. He's all for those silly-arse traditions – all that "playing fields of Eton" stuff too, isn't he? Just like long, tall Tessa. It's all old hat, you know – all yesterday's values; a bit like this stupid government we've got, which could actually be making some worthwhile changes. They've got a mandate for sweeping change and they're wasting it. Anyway, I'm willing to bet that your friend will soon come riding out of hiding – a veritable knight in shining armour, ready to rescue his damsel in distress. A dashing cavalier, who's soon to be unhorsed. Is he any good in bed, Tessa?'

'Well, there's no longer any doubt about how that train of yours works,' Tessa replied over her shoulder. 'All that hot air you generate would propel it for a week.'

'Ha ha. Very droll.' Jemima's voice had a harder edge to it now, though there was still an immature, 'giggly' undertone to it. 'I can assure you, darling, that we generate a lot more than hot air. We're making the future – and it works. Unlike the relics those time and money wasting steam societies try to keep running – using taxpayer funds in some cases – our train is no outdated romantic monstrosity, but a cutting-edge technological masterpiece. It's not just a means of mass transit, you know: it's a local security system and, if need be, a first strike weapon. I'm not about to tell you how it all works just now, of course. You'll be seeing it in action soon enough, but first you'll join your friends and fellow inmates – with a smattering of local yokels – in our compound for the night.'

Jemima was obviously enjoying herself. Though out of her preferred physical environment, she was doing what she loved best – exercising power over people and events. What she didn't know, however, was that she was being followed. Wally Steiler, moving with the stealth and wraith-like gait of a hunting dingo, was flowing between the gums and grass trees less than a hundred and fifty yards behind, and he was not prepared to let Tessa, or her two captors, out of his sight.

Chapter Fourteen
Tuesday 19th July 4.25 pm

'THAT OLD MILKIN' shed don't look much different from the last time I saw it,' Emil Steiler pronounced in a puzzled voice. He was peering through Hugh Bainbridge's telescope at a rustic, unpainted weatherboard structure which nestled on a cleared rise just a short distance from the glade where both men now lay, ensconced behind a screen of thick scrub and undergrowth.

'It's certainly no Alcatraz, is it?' Hugh suggested. 'There looks to have been a spot of carpentry done at the southern end – some sort of enclosed room or living quarters perhaps – but it would hardly hold a group of prisoners. And there are no guards about, or any signs of high security at all. Wally was saying that some tradesmen's trucks came up here a while back?'

'Yeah – they did. A concrete truck and some earth movin' equipment, as well as a builder. All outa-town tradesmen, by the look of 'em – no local blokes. There was a bit o' talk around the valley about how the new owners kept to 'emselves, and even brought in outsiders to do the work. The rumour was that they were convertin' this shed into a couple o' holiday cabins, and then layin' down some concrete slabs as a base for some new buildin's.'

'Hmm. Interesting.' Hugh began checking out the creek flats and gully entrances with his telescope. 'There doesn't seem to be much activity at all, does there? Maybe it was all for show or, just possibly, they did their main construction further afield, somewhere else on the property perhaps. I say!'

Surprised by an urgent rustle in the glade behind them, both men whirled around to meet a potential attacker, relaxing with a sharp intake of breath when they recognised the new arrival as Wally. It was a very different Wally however, from the one they had left a couple of hours earlier. The craggy honest face was now etched with deep lines of concern, while sweat had soaked the bushman's shirt and his arms were savagely scratched below the folds of his up-rolled sleeves. 'Sorry to give you blokes a fright,' he said softly. 'I been pushin' me way through bloody lantana for nearly half an hour. That gully's all over-growed with the stuff – rips buggery out o' yer arms but I had to get here as quick as I could.'

'Wally, old man – are you alright?' Hugh darted forward. 'You look as if you've been through the mill.'

'You all right, mate?' Emil reiterated, his laconic style clearly failing to mask his anxiety.

'Yeah – yeah, I'm alright.' Wally waved his arms dismissively. 'Don't you blokes go worryin' about me. It's Tess I'm worried about. Hugh – Hugh mate, I'm sorry – they've got her. She's a prisoner!'

'What? How?' Hugh's mask of reserve was also broken.

'I could bloody well kick meself, mate,' Wally almost wailed. 'I was only a few feet away in the bush. Neither of us saw it comin'. It was that bloody business executive sheila from Sydney – the one Tess knows – the one who was s'posed to have got kidnapped a couple o' weeks ago. We were both up near the edge o' the scrub when all of a sudden here comes this woman, racin' like mad up the spur, and we both thought she must have escaped from someone, and was runnin' away. So Tess dives out in the open to pull her down into cover with us. Next thing, she pulls a gun – a little pocket pistol – and points it at Tess. There I am – sittin' there in the bush – couldn't do a damn thing. I was tempted, I tell ya – I wanted to try somethin' but she had Tess hostage with a gun at her head, and if I'd gone out and called on her to throw it down, well, it would've been a stand-off, I reckon. I would've ended up havin' to put me rifle down, for Tessa's safety, and then we both would've been captured. There was another one of them comin' up the track, too, just to complicate things. Oh, I dunno if I did the right thing, but I thought if I just laid low and followed 'em, and I could get back to you blokes, we might be able to sort something out. I was tempted though, I tell ya – I reckon I could've nearly shot the gun out of her hand, I was that near, but I couldn't take the chance, what with the two women bein' that close together. I'm sorry, Hugh.'

'Wally, old chap, you did all you could.' Hugh put a reassuring hand on the bushman's shoulder. 'You did the right thing – the only possible thing under the circumstances. Now stop blaming yourself. Let's have a think now: did you see where they went?'

'Well, that's another weird bloody thing. I've lived in the bush all me life and I reckon I'm not too bad at trackin' and stalkin', all things considered. I was determined not to let 'em out of me sight, and I didn't neither – till about halfway down the mountain. They were walkin' ahead of me down the spur, you see, and I'm followin' about six or seven chain behind, keepin' to the cover wherever I could; till finally they came to a bend in the track, near a big rocky knob that sort o' runs up from the edge o' the spur. They vanished into a little belt o' scrub just near there, and they didn't come back out. After a good fifteen minutes, I decided to go in after 'em. There was a little track runnin' in through the scrub a little ways, so I follered their tracks along that, until I come up against a sheer rock wall – no track to left or right. I tell ya, I'm startin' to wonder if there is somethin' fishy about this ghost train, and the people connected with it. They seem to be able to make 'emselves, and the ones they kidnap, just disappear – into rocks, or maybe into bloody thin air!'

'Here, have a swig from the canteen, Wally,' Hugh suggested. 'Now what say you have a spell for a few minutes – have a bite of some food, old chap – and then you can show us the way back to the place where they disappeared. Between us, we might pick up some sort of clue, somewhere around that rocky knob. It's almost certain that they won't bring Tess back here – Emil and I have been having a dekko through the telescope and we're sure this place is no prison.'

'Looks like there is some bugger in there though,' Emil suddenly put in. 'See, at the window. Hello! Looks as if he's comin' outside.'

As the trio watched from their hiding place, a straw-thatched man in a khaki uniform emerged from the renovated end of the building and began a patrol of the dairy environs, eventually clambering to the top of a nearby bluff, from which vantage point he used binoculars to sweep the area from the shed to the road.

This sentry, as he appeared to be, carefully scrutinised a one ton Holden utility which hammered past the property entrance in a cloud of dust, keeping his glasses trained on the vehicle till it was a mere speck in the distance, but he did not seem at all concerned with the prospect behind him. Clearly no intruders were expected from that direction, vindicating Wally's original strategy of entering the old Muller property through the back, by crossing Cattle Mountain.

'You know, with a bit of luck, I'm inclined to think one could stalk clear up to that chap, and tap him on the shoulder,' Hugh whispered to his companions. 'He might be able to tell us something.'

'You sure, mate?' Emil looked askance at the professor, who nodded blithely. 'Well, all right, but I'll be coverin' him. The bugger's got a rifle slung across his shoulder, you know.'

Hugh quickly bent to the task, darting in a low crouched run between the sparse trees, boulders and lantana clumps which dotted the open paddock between the scrub-covered mountain foothills and the dairy shed. The sentry had seated himself on a blackened stump and was taking a draught from a stubby beer bottle when the professor spoke softly behind him.

'Tut, tut. Drinking on the job, old man? Never would have done during my days in uniform.'

'What the friggin' hell – ?' The man made a frantic grab for his rifle, but Hugh was ready for that, sending the weapon flying with an almost balletic kick. A hard right to the sentry's jaw drove him sprawling full length onto the dry grass; then, seizing a wrist, the professor dragged his foe upright with an arm pinioned behind his back.

'Now, old fellow, let's have some information,' Hugh demanded as Wally and Emil jogged up. 'Jolly quick too, if you don't mind. Where's your main headquarters – the place where you house your prisoners? Speak up, man!'

'Hang on, hang on. Leggo me arm, will ya? I'm just a bloody lookout: I dunno nothin' about the main turnout. Here, lemme sit down for a minute, on that stump. I'm not gonna run anywhere – I'll tell ya everythin' I know.'

Hugh warily released the man, who resumed his seat with his captors close about on three sides. He looked nervously from one to the other and began fishing in a tunic pocket.

'Just need some chewin' gum,' he said. 'Mouth's dry, ya know. Now look; I dunno nothin' really – 'specially 'bout what goes on up the back. Other people are s'posed to look after that area. My orders are to watch the front o' the property – just from 'ere out to the road, the creek flats, this paddock mainly – and see that no trespassers or snoopers come onto the place.'

'And where do you go when you finish your shift?' Hugh asked.

'I sleep 'ere, in that room on the end o' the dairy. Another bloke comes an' relieves me shortly, an' patrols the place all night.'

'And where does he come from?' The professor's voice was still urbane but a certain exasperation was beginning to show. 'Now listen here, man: the people you work for are kidnappers and thugs; potentially murderers. They've forcibly abducted some good people, the most recent being a very dear friend of mine. It's almost inconceivable that you don't know where their headquarters are, and you're going to be in a lot of trouble once the legitimate authorities become involved in this show. In the meantime, you could make things considerably better for yourself by guiding us to the place where any prisoners are being held. Now move!'

'No chance, mate. It's worth more than me life to take you jokers anywhere, specially with it bein' the big day tomorrow. Anyway, it's too late – that chewin' gum was more than sugar – it's a narcotic they gave us, in case this ever 'appened. I'm gonna be out – of action – for a whi – '.

The man's eyes had glassed over and he toppled over sideways off the stump. Hugh and Emil caught him and lowered the unconscious figure to the ground.

'His pulse and respiration are fine,' Hugh said, after a quick check. 'Obviously these minions have been primed and indoctrinated pretty thoroughly, and warned not to give out any information. Goodness knows what he meant by it being the big day tomorrow. Well, I suppose we'll have to carry the bloke to his living quarters inside that dairy and stow him there. We could tie him up but I suppose he'll be quickly released anyway, once the replacement sentry arrives. We might be better off just to stick him inside there and bolt.'

'Yeah, the less time we waste the better, eh?' said Wally, grabbing the sentry's ankles. Hugh took the unconscious man under the arms and they quickly transported him to the room from which he had come, placing him quite comfortably on a bunk in the corner.

'Hope they're bein' as kind to their prisoners as we are to ours,' Emil observed. 'That bloke's set up as snug as a bug in a rug.'

'Well, we couldn't leave him outside for the dingoes, I s'pose,' Wally said gruffly. 'Though maybe the ringleaders o' this turnout deserve that.'

'Well chaps, are we ready to make tracks?' said Hugh. 'We've an hour or so of daylight left. Perhaps we can find a way into the lair of these blackguards by retracing your steps, Wally – back up to that rocky knob.'

They filed out into the freshening afternoon air and marched back toward the mountainside, unaware that their movements were even now being observed. In a nearby copse of trees, a smartly uniformed Constable Ben Baker of the Mirambeena police laid down a pair of field glasses and picked up a walkie-talkie.

'WELCOME TO OUR field headquarters, Tessa,' Jemima Blackman announced. 'Or at least, the outdoor section of it, known to some of us as *Camp Diablo*. You'll notice our compound and exercise yard, railway workshops and a couple of demountable administration buildings. There's a lot more underground of course: that's where the real 'wizardry' – or should I say 'chemistry' – is located.'

Tessa was marching down a giddying series of cliff-hugging stone steps, with Jemima behind her and the man called Herman a few paces ahead. The path wound down into a deep mountainside depression, which had been scooped out – using the obvious aid of sophisticated earthmoving equipment – into a bowl-like crater perhaps two hundred metres in diameter. Glancing up and around as they continued their descent, Tess quickly realised why the basin and its man-made structures had not been visible from Cattle Mountain or the Jump-Up, for both the western and eastern escarpments were crested by jutting pinnacles or hillocks: anything behind or below these natural battlements would be concealed from almost any vantage point.

The basin was apparently drained by two steep and narrow ravines, which fell away to either side of the eastern wall and plunged on down the mountainside, their courses mostly hidden by tangled trees and undergrowth. Access to these gullies, and to a gaping tunnel in the base of the wall was, however, clearly barred by high, electrified steel grating. Dense forest framed the entire southern lip of the crater, while to the north, above and behind the descending trio, a thick belt of scrub fringing the ledge gave way eventually to the great rocky knob where Wally had lost their tracks. It was still hard to believe, looking back up the stairway, that they had actually come *through* that vast reef of granite and limestone into this hidden valley. For Tess, that had been the biggest surprise of all: that incredible moment when a portion of the rock face had simply opened up before them. Like a scene lifted from an old matinee serial, a steel lever concealed by vines had been tripped, and a vast stone 'door' had revolved inwards – to reveal a tunnel leading straight through the outcrop to the steps they were now descending.

Again you had to hand it to these people: it was a stunning feat of engineering and it was difficult on one level not to acknowledge the skills which had been employed. On the other side of the ledger, however, were the underlying criminality and utterly ruthless conduct of the gang, and their obviously sinister, if still un-revealed, aims and purposes. At least, Tess considered, there was *one* positive side – knowledge of the enemy's position. Now that she was standing on the inside, the motives of this ratbag group might soon become clear, and with night approaching, an opportunity to escape might eventually present itself ; although by the look of those craggy, high-lipped basin walls and electrified fences, getting out of this hole in the hillside was not going to be easy.

'I wouldn't even think about it, if I were you.'

Jemima's crisp voice broke suddenly into Tessa's reverie. 'Climbing those walls would be an open invitation to get picked off by one of our sentries, and these steps we're on, like all other exits, are under constant surveillance. Besides, Tessa, I'd like to have a little talk with you later this evening: I'll have to discuss the matter with my chief associates first of course, but I believe I can make you a very attractive business proposal.'

'You must be joking,' was the lawyer's reply. 'I'd just as soon do business with General Franco or Idi Amin.'

'Now don't be too hasty, darling,' Jemima cooed. 'A brilliant legal mind like yours should never rush to judgment. Anyway, see how you feel after a spell in the compound. You may change your tune when you realise what the alternatives are.'

They had arrived at the foot of the terraced stairway and ahead lay a flat expanse of cleared ground, a large portion of which was enclosed by a wooden stockade. The man Herman sprinted ahead and in response to his barked commands, a large gate swung inward to allow access to the enclosure.

'Go ahead,' Jemima ordered, motioning with her pistol toward the compound entrance. 'Join your co-workers inside. You should know at least one of them already and I dare say, given your friendly, unassuming nature, that you'll soon become acquainted with the rest.'

Fighting off a sudden sense of apprehension, which she took great care to conceal from Jemima, Tessa shrugged her shoulders and marched through the gate into a parched, dust-swept courtyard, framed at one end by several sheds and demountable huts, and dotted here and there with large iron plates, steel billets, outdoor work benches, anvils and a forge.

Clustered around, or trudging between, these scattered items of hardware were some twenty-five or thirty workers. Though varying considerably in age, build and complexion, these prisoners were attired uniformly in bright orange overalls, no doubt to afford easy recognition and to present vivid outlines to the armed, khaki-clad sentries standing on parapets around the compound walls. Lurid, stark and utterly authoritarian, the nickname *Camp Diablo* seemed at once ironic and thoroughly apt.

While they all looked tired and unenthusiastic about the tasks of brazing, welding, lifting and carrying in which they were engaged, every member of the work gang looked up to appraise the latest arrival in the compound, and the face of one young prisoner broke into a bitter-sweet smile of recognition.

'Tessa!' Angela Reimann called out, dropping the cast iron bar she had been dragging. 'What are you doing here? Don't tell me they got you too.'

'Hi, Angie,' Tessa replied, throwing her arms around the girl's shoulders. 'For the moment, yes: I'm here with you guys. But let me tell you, I've got some friends on the outside – and not too far away, hopefully. With any sort of luck, the cavalry might soon be arriving.' Tessa knew she was exuding an air of confidence that she could not rationally justify; but she had summed up Angela from their first meeting as someone of considerable courage, inclined to respond to any message of hope. With luck, any new-found optimism would quickly radiate out to the other prisoners – and right now they all looked as if they needed a dose. Furthermore, Tess knew that she had to be quick in spreading the word, for one of the guards was already shouting a pointed warning through a megaphone.

'Reimann! Get away from that new person: get back to your work!'

The harsh command elicited nothing more than a cheeky grin from Angela, and Tess knew as the girl strolled back to her iron bar that she had got her message across. If the time came to call on these people to rebel, there was a better than even chance that at least one would respond.

Chapter Fifteen
Tuesday 19th July 6.15pm

'LOOK: HERE'S WHERE their tracks went – straight into the bloody rock!' Walter Steiler played the beam of a small torch along a leaf-strewn, scrub-walled pathway, revealing three distinct sets of footprints which ended abruptly at a towering rock face. A fourth set of tracks, which Wally identified as his own, could also be seen on the narrow jungle corridor which Hugh and the Steiler brothers were now exploring.

'As you say, Wally, they don't appear to have diverged off the track, either to right or left.' The professor was glancing around as he spoke. 'The scrub on either side looks all but impenetrable; and climbing that rock wall ahead looks out of the question. It's sheer.'

'Maybe there's a gap or crack in it somewhere,' Emil suggested.

'Buggered if I could see anything when I was here before,' said Wally. 'An' that was daylight. But let's have another look.'

The three men probed and pushed at several suspicious looking fissures and grooves in the rock face, but by no amount of combined shoving, jerking or other applications of brute force could any portion of the edifice be made to budge. After several minutes of fruitless exertion, they paused to draw breath.

'We'll have to find another way over or around this outcrop,' Hugh announced. 'I'm assuming that there's another gully, or ravine of some sort, beyond this rock wall. Is there an easier way to drop over into it, further back up the mountain?'

'Yeah: this reef flattens out further up the spur, but then the scrub is hellishin' thick, and we'd probably make a lot o' noise breakin' through. As I recall it, that depression on the other side is like a big basin, with two narrow gullies drainin' it at the bottom. It's really deep and treacherous too – haven't been into it for years but it's like a big hole in the mountainside, with steep, rocky cliffs formin' the walls, all hidden by scrub-covered overhangs.'

'Hmm. We'll have to be careful – sounds like a dangerous place to venture into at night.' Hugh whistled apprehensively. 'Perhaps if we just try to crawl through the scrub, inching our way along with your little torch to guide us, Wally.'

'That'd be the best way. Those cliffs could be a hundred foot high. In the dark, it'd be just so easy to topple over and smash yourself up – or worse.'

Soberly, the three men retraced their steps back along the scrub-girded track, away from the rock wall and out onto the lightly-treed spur, where they trudged off up a well-worn cattle pad. After climbing perhaps a hundred paces to get above the rock outcrop, they got down on all fours and gingerly pushed into the thick scrub, aware that a sheer drop into a yawning abyss lay concealed somewhere – possibly only a few metres – ahead.

Fifteen minutes of nerve-wracking, physically arduous crawling, which had each man sweating despite the evening's chill, at last brought them out into the open. The flood of welcome moonlight which greeted the trio, however, served to baffle rather than enlighten them. 'It's gone!' Wally Steiler gazed around as if awe-struck. 'That bloody big basin has gone!'

The bushman was right. Instead of a chasm or vast hole in the mountainside, a gently undulating plateau, peppered with grassy tussocks, billowed up before them.

'I tell ya; a man's goin' bloody mad.' Warily, as if the ground before him might turn out to be a mirage, or a thin membrane ready to collapse beneath his feet, Wally ambled forward, followed by Hugh and Emil. 'This is just bloody ridiculous. There used ter be a big hole here. Either that, or I can't find me way 'round the hills anymore; maybe me sense o' direction is off, or me memory's playin' tricks. Let's go back down the mountain and see if we can find those two narrer gullies.'

This they swiftly did, but the ravines also looked different in the moonlight, their upper ends barred by slabs of sheer rock. Somehow, the whole character of the mountainside had changed.

'I hate to say it, but I'm bushed. I dunno what's goin' on.' Wally's brow knitted furiously as he spoke. 'I'm startin' to wonder if we should maybe hole up in the scrub on the other side o' the spur for a while; near where Tess and I were hidin' when that woman first came along. We could maybe snatch a bit o' rest; then at first light we could venture over this way an' see if we can find out where on earth they've all got to. In daylight, we can comb the whole flamin' mountain – and maybe somehow work out what the hell is goin' on.'

Every fibre of Hugh's being wanted to protest, but the commonsense of Wally's proposal was manifest. Reluctantly the three men again began retracing their steps up the spur. Behind them meantime, ensconced in a tangle of undergrowth, Constable Ben Baker was carefully studying their movements. One of the policeman's hands was fingering the butt of his revolver, while the other toyed nervously with a two way radio.

Tuesday 19th July 7.45pm

A LUMINESCENCE THAT resembled moonlight was lending an almost surreal radiance to the crater beyond the rock wall. It was now a vast, shimmering, de-Chirico-esque tableau, with something of Ernst in the anvils, forges and hammers, and also in the huge iron plates being welded together by gangs of orange-suited workers. The vast stadium-style roof, which had blossomed out from the highest edges of the basin just after nightfall, clearly contained fluorescent elements in its structure, imbuing the nocturne below with a strange metaphysical ambience that highlighted the rigid geometry of the stockade and the army of slow, almost robotic figures trudging mechanically between tasks.

Some of the prisoners had been rostered off for a meal break and among this fortunate few sat Tessa, next to a young man who introduced himself as Angie Reimann's boyfriend.

'Hi, Warren; it's so good to meet you at last,' the lawyer said, shaking hands. 'I suppose you realise you've become pretty famous: you've been in all the newspapers.'

'Yeah. I s'pose that'd be right.' The young man grinned – a slow smile that seemed to arrive with difficulty from a distant time and a far-off place. It was gratifying to find him sound in both mind and limb, although his spirits were clearly down and his face looked careworn and fatigued.

'I tell ya, Tessa,' he said quietly. 'I didn't know what struck me, the night that train first showed up. I could only think about gettin' the car off the track, eh? – and then I tried to bolt. A sort o' gassy smell hit me then an' I remember staggerin' along the edge o' the tracks – I should have gone for the bush but I was kind o' disoriented. I lost one o' me shoes – well, thongs they were actually – an' then I looked up an' here's this big joker, leanin' halfway out o' the train. I remember tryin' to swing a punch at him but he was a big strong bugger an' he just grabbed me – scooped me up, sort o' thing. I've seen him around this place a few times since – he even comes in wearin' a suit sometimes – seems to be one o' the bosses o' the turnout.'

'Arblaster,' Tessa said knowingly.

'I think that is his name, yeah. Well, he's always talkin' to that blonde bird – the bossy one, ya know.'

'Yes, I know exactly who you mean,' Tessa wrinkled her nose. 'Tell me, Warren: do you have any idea what all this construction and metal work is in aid of?'

'Not really. Some of it is apparently reinforcement for the train carriages – sort o' like armour plating – and there's other bits o' special equipment – storage vats and such like – for the train. They don't tell us much o' course – we're just basically slave labour – but there's a big rush job on now, which has to be finished by tomorrer. They been fair floggin' us to get it all done – lit'rally in some cases – so we all reckon it must be some big thing they're gonna use the train for. They want it all ready by first light in the mornin'. If it's not finished, there'll be hell to pay, they reckon.'

'And there will.' Responding from the sidelines came a voice like quicksilver, flowing and glittering with juvenile enthusiasm yet bitter and metallic in its essence. 'However, I must correct you on your 'slave labour' assertion, Mr Schultz. Do a good job now and you people are all going to benefit in the long run. Benefit big time – if you can imagine that! The opportunities, for people who show some enterprise, will be astonishing.'

Jemima Blackman, clad in a rich blue cat-suit which highlighted her undeniably curvaceous figure, stepped into the light and sat down on an outdoor table now scattered with soup bowls. 'Well, Tessa,' she said with a grin. 'You've now seen something of our little show; how we guide and coax people toward high achievement. You'll see the old *Diablo* arrive shortly, to be fitted with all these toys and embellishments. It's going to be unstoppable, you know. Anyway, that brings me to my point. Come with me now and meet my business partners. I think we may be able to put something your way; something at once challenging, stimulating and financially rewarding. It's right up your street professionally, too.'

'I thought I made it clear that I wasn't interested in any of your proposals,' Tessa said firmly. 'I don't do business with criminals.'

'Oh, come on now: don't dismiss anything out of hand. Besides, within a few days we won't be considered criminals – quite the reverse, I'd be willing to wager.'

'I'm not budging.'

'Well then, you leave me no alternative. If you're not prepared to come and listen to a perfectly reasonable business proposition, and to discuss some areas where you can apply your skills in guiding the future of this nation, then I'm afraid that I too will have to demonstrate iron resolve – temporarily and in a strictly limited way, of course. I am now going to shed some staff – you know, dispense with some redundant labour. Hmm. Let's see now: whom shall we select?' Jemima directed her gaze toward two figures brazing metal rods at a nearby forge.

'Ah! I doubt we'll get much more work out of those two tonight. Oh, aren't they your girlfriend's parents – the Reimanns? What a shame.' She turned coldly toward Warren Schultz who, like Tessa, was rising quickly to his feet.

'Dear me! Your future in-laws. Oh well, that can't be helped. Herman! Herman!'

As the uniformed man rushed up, Jemima gestured toward the pair she had just selected as victims.

'Get rid of them,' she snapped. 'Take them down to the gas tanks; not up here.'

'Wait!' Tessa almost yelled. 'I'll talk to you. I might as well hear what you have to say.' She shot a warning look back at Warren, who seemed on the point of launching a physical assault on either Herman or Jemima. The latter chuckled as the young fellow took Tessa's hint and sat back down, though his face was contorted with barely suppressed rage.

'Good move, Tessa,' Jemima laughed. 'That village idiot was about to get himself shot.'

The two women walked off to a nearby building, a one room demountable structure with a board table and several comfortable chairs at its centre. The fluorescent tubes which lighted this field office, like the heating system that warmed it, were obviously powered by a generator hammering away outside the window, a device which apparently supplied sufficient electricity to also send periodic floodlight beams arcing around the crater. It was hard to tell whether the same engine was responsible for the soft glow which emanated from the roof: clearly, there were all sorts of engineering marvels around, including those which could quickly turn a large pit in the hillside into a vast underground cavern, so that work could proceed at night without the risk of lights being seen. In the daytime, Tess realised, this would hardly be a problem, as the natural barriers at either end of the crater, coupled with the thick scrub and granite outcrops along its flanks, would generally prevent anyone from looking in. All told, this was quite a sound and secure looking set-up, run with clear and ruthless efficiency by people who appeared fully confident of maintaining order within, while avoiding detection from without.

'Take a seat,' Jemima Blackman offered. 'Like a drink, Tessa? We run to the odd bottle of good white, despite being stuck out here in the middle of hillbilly-ville.'

'No thanks,' Tessa said curtly.

'Suit yourself. Look Tessa, why don't you just relax? You're not going anywhere in a hurry, so you might as well hear our proposals with an open and receptive mind. We are, after all, talking about charting a completely new direction for the whole country: a path towards undreamt of prosperity which will benefit everyone – and, as you might have gathered, we have now reached something of a pivotal point in the journey.'

'I'm listening,' Tessa said. 'Delusions of grandeur on this scale need to be aired. Your exposition should make for an interesting psychological case study.'

'I'll overlook the cynicism, Tessa, because you don't as yet understand the big picture, the sheer scale of what's about to happen, or even the micro detail – in short, the practical strategies required to effect lasting and worthwhile change. You need to realise that this is no mere parochial issue, or locally-focused movement: our agenda in fact goes right to the heart of things at a national level. You see, we believe that the old ways simply don't cut the mustard anymore. We need a completely new framework, a reformed and strengthened system of governance – a system controlled firmly from the centre, by practical business-minded people. That's where you come in.'

'Really?'

'Yes. Let's face it, Tess: you're both a brilliant advocate and a formidable legal drafter. You've advised both state and federal governments on constitutional and administrative matters. Now we need to draft a whole new constitution, a new criminal code, a new legislative and regulatory structure – the international community, as well as our own law makers, will recognise nothing less. It means starting from scratch, with a clean sheet of paper, and it will require the input of focused, analytical minds – like yours. We'll want a system which locks out any input from union thugs, parasitic welfare bludgers, old agrarian socialists, or the trendy left inhabitants of the universities, but we'll want the whole show to be founded on a watertight, codified system of law.'

'What's wrong with our present framework?' Tessa attempted a reasoned approach, albeit with little expectation of success. 'We have all sorts of built-in safeguards … traditional freedoms …

conventions. The entrepreneur can make money; there are protections for wage earners to prevent exploitation; *and* there's a safety net for those who need it.'

'Uh uh!' Jemima shook her head fiercely. 'We need to shift the balance, Tess – shift it firmly and irrevocably in favour of the productive ones. *They* need to be in charge, guiding and directing those who lack the initiative, the will or the intelligence to improve their own lot. We need to remove all constraints – anything that stands in the way of making a profit – and in the long run, this deregulated environment will create a trickle-down effect, so that those at the bottom of the pile, if you like, will also reap the benefits. They'll learn how to freely negotiate their own contracts, and become the architects of their own rewards.'

'I see. Just like those people in the compound are doing?'

'Oh well, that's a demonstration of sorts.' The businesswoman waved a hand dismissively. 'Workers will have to realise, Tessa, that at the start of any new enterprise they will not be able to harbour high expectations or make false demands. The laws of the market are clear and inviolable: until profitability is reached – or, for that matter, if profitability should falter in an established business – people should be prepared to work for whatever is offered by those charged with managerial responsibility. It may simply be food, shelter and clothing, as we are currently providing; or alternatively they can look elsewhere for a job, or fall back on their own resources.'

Tessa's eyes blazed. 'What hypocrisy! You're not allowing these people to look for alternative employment. In fact, some of them already have it. You've kidnapped them – torn them from their homes, families and occupations.'

'Well, of course, the analogy is imperfect. This operation here is not a business enterprise *per se*. It's a revolution, if you like, and in a revolution some people have to make sacrifices, in order to achieve worthwhile and lasting benefits for the majority. It's abundantly clear that centralised authority is the only way to go, without all these inefficient divisions and diversions – this quagmire of states, tribunals, commissions, select committees, enquiries; so much needless opposition and debate. The time for all that is past. Firm decisions, taken by a far-sighted, enlightened executive, must flow unimpeded, from the top down, for the benefit of all. Australia is going to be a model for the rest of the world, Tess – the first nation to be governed solely by an enterprise class; the first genuinely free society on earth.'

'Free? It hardly sounds like it. Through your top-down, centralised system, you apparently intend to eliminate any freedom to formulate alternative viewpoints or philosophies. Where are the means to express different ideas – through political parties, an official opposition or independent representatives? What about input from professional and producer organisations, and trade unions? Where are the safeguards – the checks and balances?'

'Oh, we'll allow political parties; but they'll need to be supervised and guided, by an electoral commission with teeth, to ensure that they're focused on the important things – such as wealth creation, road planning, and improvements to infrastructure. The Prime Minister, advised by a Cabinet drawn directly from the business community, will exercise strong and resolute authority. Local representatives will act as a conduit, to convey decisions back to the punters, but the hard choices have to be made by those with proven leadership ability – people with enterprise, who know how to make a profit. Our present problems are all due to having too many restraints on such people, too much red tape – too many checks and balances in fact. The crown, the states, the courts, the unions – they're all anachronisms now. People need direction, and the only way to achieve that is a firm, guiding hand at the centre: *one* head of power, and only one!'

'I see. And how do you propose to bring this new system into being? I gather your plans don't include any sort of free vote or referendum.'

'Well, hardly! As I've just been pointing out, the average punter needs guidance, clear sign-posting and, at times, even a bit of prodding. The man or woman in the street could hardly be trusted with a decision on something as important as this. No, I'm afraid the new order must be imposed, for the good of everyone. And it's already a virtual *fait accompli*. People will readily accept it, once they see the present Prime Minister, and at least two state premiers, capitulating and accepting our terms for a smooth transfer of power.'

'What? Are you completely and utterly mad?'

'Quite the contrary. You'd have to be mad to oppose us. And people won't attempt to, once they realise our capabilities. You may remember this afternoon, Tess, that I hinted at our train's potential as a mobile security system and a first strike platform. By tomorrow, those abilities will all be enhanced ten fold and the *Diablo* itself will be a virtual rolling fortress – impregnable, unstoppable – thanks to the efforts of that happy little gang of Vegemites out there in the compound. I won't say they've been totally willing, but enough of them have been able, and the result is that they've finished all the manufacturing tasks that we've set them. All that's needed now is to fit the modifications – armour plating for the *Diablo*'s carriages, a giant battering ram for the loco's nose and large, sealed, triple-reinforced gas tanks, which will ride in purpose-built cabins on purpose-built rolling stock.

Jemima paused for effect, as if addressing a shareholders' meeting.

'Oh, you're probably unaware of our gas-manufacturing facilities – one of the side benefits of employing a couple of the country's top industrial chemists.' The businesswoman smiled broadly. 'They already worked for my company, so they weren't too hard to bring on board. Let me just explain that our train will carry two types of gas. One is a rather smelly methane compound, which your friend the romantic professor would have got a whiff of the other afternoon: we were just trialling it from a small drum then. In the right concentrations and quantities however, it could temporarily incapacitate a whole street; have them sneezing and falling about all over the place. We'll use that one first as a bit of a primer – a shot across the bows so to speak.'

'And the other?'

'Oh, just sarin nerve gas.' Jemima actually giggled as she spoke. 'We may not have to use it, of course, but in case anyone is inclined to refuse our demands, a quick demonstration of its effects should convince them that we mean business. We also have equipment ready to pipe it up here into the compound – if anyone did somehow happen to delay or baulk us, we'll be in regular radio contact with base and the message will quickly go through to use it on these prisoners.'

A chill ran down Tessa's spine. A small-time bunch of militant free-marketeers, randomly taking hostages and operating in league with corrupt law enforcement officers, was a bad enough scenario, but these people were clearly playing for far higher stakes than she had originally suspected. They were terrorists, zealots and extremists of the most dangerous sort, determined to impose their particular brand of dictatorship on the populace at large and prepared to use any means of force to achieve their aims.

Slowly, almost imperceptibly, Tess glanced around. Escape was looking more and more difficult. Extra guards were appearing outside, while Maurice Arblaster and Inspector Jensen now joined herself and Jemima inside the room – yet it seemed more important than ever to find out the exact nature of the group's plans.

'What makes you think the Prime Minister, or any of the Premiers, will accede to your demands?' she asked the businesswoman. 'It's not their habit to give in to threats or intimidation.'

Jemima laughed. 'They'll find it hard to refuse, as they'll be in our custody. You may not be aware, especially if you've been out of touch with daddy for a while, that his esteemed leader Mr Fraser will soon be arriving in this very region. The Prime Minister, it seems, is paying a visit to the little Darling Downs city of Warumbah, to attend a scientific conference, along with the Premiers of both Queensland and New South Wales. Our sources tell us that big Mal will be using the opportunity to discuss interstate transport issues with both Nifty

Nev and old redneck Joh; and, ironically enough, rail freight is going to be one of the main topics of conversation. Well, won't they all get a surprise when *our* train – the good old *Diablo* – rumbles into town to deliver its cargo tomorrow?'

'Tomorrow!' Tess exclaimed.

'That's right. As I said, all the manufacturing work has already been completed, and we have a night shift organised which will carry out the necessary modifications, equipping the *Diablo* with all the items of offence and defence that it needs to deflect an army. They'd need giant artillery to stop us; but long before they could even think of deploying that sort of firepower, we will have made our strike, taken our VIP hostages *and* staged our coup. Game over!'

'You'd go overland to Warumbah?' Tessa wondered, finding her voice a little shaky. 'Or via a tunnel?'

'Unfortunately, we don't have a tunnel running in that direction. Our underground rail system currently extends from the old coal mines near Rinehart's Ridge, to just below our present position. But it's hardly a problem – we'll simply take the most direct cross-country route through the ranges. You see, it's not really that far, as the bird flies, to Warumbah, and as most people think the *Diablo* is some sort of apparition and don't believe in its material existence, I doubt that anyone will raise any sort of credible alarm. Any reports of the train travelling overland in broad daylight will, as usual, be laughed off.'

'You see, sweetheart,' Inspector Jensen's oily voice now broke in, 'that's been the beauty of the whole thing. Our strike vehicle is based on a dicky old local legend, and sightings can easily be dismissed as bullshit by the authorities – our authorities! We've been able to take control of, and keep the lid on, any official investigation of individual incidents, and ridicule any outside reportage as mere sensationalism. We've avoiding nabbing any really important people – you know, ones with connections who might stir up a fuss – and we've kept our conscripted work force mainly to local yokels and the odd blow-in. Oh, we've had to keep a good eye on the district and lean on a few people who got nosey: unfortunately though, some people can't take a hint; they keep stickin' their beaks in.' He leered meaningly at Tessa.

'The other beautiful thing,' suggested Maurice Arblaster, 'has been the sheer efficiency of the technology we've employed. Our train may look like an antiquated throwback to another era but, as you've no doubt come to realise, it has engineering features far in advance of any transportation system currently on the drawing board. It can run on tracks like a conventional steam train; using a linear induction system it can levitate and then hover along sections of track equipped with magnets – we are presently trialling this technology in our tunnels; and by using a recently-perfected, cutting edge steering system, it can also travel overland. The latter is the real *piece de resistance* of course, because it turns a train – a transport system capable of carrying hundreds, even thousands, of people – into the ultimate go-anywhere, off-road vehicle. And the latter part is all my design: for years I've worked on plans for a coal powered, steam driven levitation system that could lift a train clear of the tracks – set it free of any restrictions – and then let it hover off, on a virtual cushion of steam, over any terrain. This twenty-first century system, I may say, is now a reality: the only drawback is that the hovering system does use a lot of coal and thus we don't use it all the time; we still run on tracks whenever they're available.'

'How do you get it up out of this crater?' Tessa's gaze ran wonderingly around the almost sheer sides of the basin. 'Surely you don't levitate up over the walls.'

'No, that would be a bit beyond even the *Diablo*'s capabilities,' Arblaster replied, beaming at the lawyer's apparent interest in his brainchild. 'As you'll see tomorrow morning, there's another side tunnel to the south, through the crater wall, which has a lesser gradient. We'll proceed via that tunnel, come up onto a spur, ascend along the spur to the ridge-top and cross not far from the peak of Cattle Mountain. Getting down into that next valley is actually a bit tricky – the south-western slopes are too scrub-choked and cut by narrow, rocky gullies – which is why we head north almost to the peak: from there we usually take a zig-zag course down the mountainside, keeping clear of the thicker scrub and more or less floating over humps and shallower gullies. Once we're down to the creek, it's off along the road for a bit, then up into the next lot of ranges, once again avoiding the scrub and the deeper gullies. Of course, after we get up onto the Downs, it's pretty smooth sailing all the way to Warumbah – a mere half-hour run, in fact.'

'And that's where our troops will take command,' added Jensen, 'and ensure a smooth transition of power. They'll all know their stuff: most of 'em are ex-mercenaries, ex-army, or former coppers from all over the place, and they're equipped with gas masks, protective suits and all the latest riot gear. I doubt anyone will be silly enough to resist – particularly after we snatch the PM and the two Premiers from under their noses – but if they try anything on, our blokes will know exactly what to do.'

'So, Tess,' said Jemima, savouring to the full a prolonged sip of white wine. 'You can see there's no point in arguing. It's a done deal, kiddo; are you in?'

'No Jemima, I'm not,' Tessa said firmly. 'I could never use my professional skills, such as they are, to prop up a regime like the one you're proposing. Call me old-fashioned, but I still happen to believe in democracy and individual rights – in a system where power is divided and constrained, not centralised in one area or person – in a society with checks and countervailing forces.'

Jemima shook her head in apparent disgust. 'It's the same old story you're sprouting, Tessa. What beats me is – why? Why would any intelligent person not go for efficiency, and for a system which is decisive and swift?'

'Perhaps it's got something to do with what Lord Acton said – that power tends to corrupt and absolute power corrupts absolutely.'

'Poppycock! Look at this clown in Canberra. He's been given a huge mandate and he's wasting it. He should be moving to crush the unions and all the welfare bludgers. Instead of that, he's out appeasing aboriginal groups – giving land away to them – in between subsidising unproductive farmers, like the scrub rats dotted around these hills.'

'That's another reason I could never support your cause, Jemima. I believe in difference and cultural diversity; in a range of traditions; in the value of age-old skills and regional knowledge; in ongoing, timeless connections with the land. Don't you get any sense of that at all out here, in these hills?'

'Pahh! The only time this countryside will be of any value is when it becomes civilised – when the scrub is bulldozed down; when it has townhouses, and condominiums, and efficient industry; and when all the unproductive, subsidised hillbillies are cleared off it. Of course, we've already started on that process – we've nabbed a few of them and have them working here in the compound. That will be the future for cockies like them.'

'I see.' Tessa's tone was sardonic. 'Just like that, eh?'

'It's the only way. Of course, in the long run, all agricultural and pastoral activity will be run by super efficient, privately-owned corporations – that's inevitable. The family farm – oh yes, and *your* old landed gentry too – they've all had their day. But, let me say, within the modern entrepreneurial society, there will be an important place for drafters and framers of legal codes – the role I was suggesting to you earlier, Tess – because we'll need a sound basis of law and order. We'll need a strong legal framework, both to keep control of the punters and to provide direction for the political parties, the executive, and the minimal – and I do stress *minimal* – public service that will be required to administer things. A totally de-regulated business sector will take care of most things, but we'll naturally need a strong police force and army to keep the populace in check.'

'So you want to *deregulate* and fully empower the corporate sector, while you *regulate* everyone else to the nth degree. A sort of business fascism, if you will. Well Jemima, my final answer is of course an absolute, rock solid, ironclad N.O. – no. I'll throw in my lot with decent people, with people of integrity and honesty – qualities which these *scrub rats*, as you call them, have in abundance. Oh, and I'm also willing to bet that most good old-fashioned capitalists won't have a bar of your new system either, once they hear what it's all about.'

'Oh, don't wager too much on that, darling,' Jemima retorted. 'We have several top business execs already involved financially, and there are quite a few more ready and willing to come on board, just as soon as we show our hands.'

'Ah, you're wasting your time with her, Jemima,' Arblaster snorted. 'Typical mealy-mouthed, silver-tail lawyer.'

The latter remark drew a chuckle from Inspector Jensen, and another quick jibe at Tessa.

'She's a regular, real life Nancy Drew, that's what she is. Well, let's see how the girl wonder likes labouring out in the compound, eh?' He guffawed loudly and leaned back in his chair.

Jemima drained her wine glass. 'Well, it's a shame you won't see reason, Tessa, because despite our differences, I always had a sort of liking for you.

You have a certain style, when you're in city mode, and you've certainly got intellectual credibility – it's just misdirected towards the romantic instead of the practical, unfortunately. Anyway, in the final analysis, all your resistance to change, your noble speeches, your worn-out traditional values – all any of them are going to get you is an orange boiler suit. They're not exactly a fashion statement, but there should be one there to fit your tall, well-bred figure.'

'Let's get on with it then.' Innumerable interviews with irascible clients, tough negotiation meetings and dispute settlement sessions, along with years of martial arts training, had all taught Tessa the value of ignoring taunts, of keeping a cool head and seizing the initiative. She now rose casually to her feet, favouring the trio at the table with an aloof sidelong glance as she started for the door.

'I could use some fresh air!' The words were tossed back over the lawyer's shoulder as she strode out into the night, effectively forcing her red-faced captors to choose between following their prisoner or remaining dumbstruck where they were, staring at each other across the table. Tess allowed herself the luxury of a slight smile as Jemima's strident voice eddied across the compound.

'Herman. Herman, you idiot. Get this prisoner over to stores and into a uniform. And make sure she does plenty of bloody work!'

Chapter Sixteen
Tuesday 19th July 8.15pm

WITH THE INNATE directional sense of an experienced bushman, Wally Steiler had guided Hugh and Emil back up the mountain spur to the exact spot at the edge of the scrub where he and Tessa had hidden before the approach of Jemima and Herman. There, just off the track amidst a tangle of lantana, wait-a-while thorns and liana cords, Wally knelt and reached a hand inside a fallen log that was virtually concealed by shrubbery.

'I stuck Tessa's gun into this holler trunk,' he explained, retrieving the Browning and pushing off downwards into the ravine with a rifle in one hand and a shotgun in the other. 'How about I take it apart now, stick a bit o' oil on it, and stash it in a hessian bag. I can always stick it back in the same place, unless we find another holler tree down here in the gully.'

'Good work, Wally.' Hugh was scraping aside leafage to make a bare patch on the gully floor, which he then surrounded with stones and filled with dry kindling. 'I think we could risk a fire, don't you – for warmth and a billy of tea?'

'Yeah; we'll need somethin' to keep us goin',' said Emil. 'I doubt the buggers will see it down here.'

'Well, we've got a few more hessian bags that we

can wrap round ourselves,' Wally suggested. 'An' we got our coats on. If we huddle round the fire, we shouldn't freeze. An' we've still got some biscuits and fruit, so we won't starve neither.'

'Thanks to you, Wally, we've got a pretty secure bolthole for the night,' Hugh ventured. 'There's a chance that guard down at the old dairy has been discovered by now but I doubt they'll want to come blundering all over the mountainside in the dark looking for us. With any sort of luck, our whereabouts should remain unknown, at least until morning.'

In that respect they were mistaken however. Someone was indeed aware of their approximate position, and the homely smell of their fire was to him a considerable source of envy. Constable Ben Baker, shivering as he huddled in a thicket just two hundred yards away, still bore the hallmarks of a man in a quandary, unsure whether to use the walkie-talkie in his hand to summon assistance, or to draw the revolver at his hip and sneak up on the men in the gully.

For the time being at least, he would opt to do neither, choosing instead to remain in what he considered an advantageous position: teeth chattering but an otherwise silent sentinel, he shivered in his jacket and kept his own counsel. He seemed as surprised as the men he was stalking when the very ground beneath him began to shake, pulsing with the sound and movement of heavy machinery. The disturbance, however, was fleeting: within a few minutes, only the call of night birds broke the silence of the mountainside.

FROM A PIT deep in the mountainside the *Spirit of Diablo* came hissing and clanking up into the crater. Soon it was trundling through a hastily-opened gateway into the compound, and forging between rows of orange-suited figures who converged – albeit with obvious reluctance – upon its steaming flanks.

'Garn! Get a move on, you lot,' the guard called Herman barked. 'Or I'll get amongst ya with a stockwhip. Get them iron plates up against the sides o' those carriages and bolt 'em into the slots. Go on, Shultz – you're s'posed to be a bloody mechanic. You can see how they're s'posed to fit on. Here you – Miss Smart Alec lawyer! Give him a hand.'

Tessa, now clad in one of the garish orange uniforms worn by all the compound prisoners, moved forward to assist Warren Schultz, along with a thirty-ish, bespectacled man who identified himself as Wesley Smythe, the Toowoomba schoolteacher whose disappearance had made the papers on the day of Tessa's arrival in Queensland. Between the three of them, they manoeuvred one of the inch-thick steel plates onto a pair of fork-lift blades, then mounted step ladders to position and bolt the armour panelling securely to one of the carriage sides.

'The darn thing's going to be impenetrable,' Wesley Smythe panted. 'First they use it as a kidnap vehicle, and now they're using us – their captives – to turn it into some sort of war machine. What's the game? What the hell is their object?'

'Power,' Tess replied. 'Authoritarian, doctrinaire, absolute control. Ironically, it's all being done in the name of free enterprise, but the methods are those of state terrorism.' And yet even as she said it, a countervailing idea was forming in the lawyer's mind. If this rolling leviathan could be an instrument of capture, of subjugation and oppression, perhaps it could also serve as a means of escape. If one could somehow slip on board during the night, and stay hidden, it might just be possible to ride this train to freedom – or a fair shot at it. If a stowaway could only remain undetected long enough to get clear of this barren crater and out onto the mountain slopes, there would at least be a decent chance. Once out there on the spurs and ridges, with scrub and narrow gullies and wood land on every side, the odds of successfully making a break, of gaining cover, and of finding help, would all increase enormously. It had to be worth a try.

Tess knew that to have any prospect of avoiding detection, she would have to jettison the luminous garb of the compound and revert to darker colours. She had been careful to note the storage shed where her slacks, shirt and parka had been thrown – no doubt to await disposal – and she now resolved to effect an entry there at the first opportunity. Of course it was hard to predict what circumstances might arise during the night. Her work gang might be relieved by a new shift and allowed to sleep; or alternatively they might be forced to work through until daybreak. It would clearly be a matter of watching, waiting and seizing the right moment, as and when it came.

Chapter Seventeen
Wednesday 20th July – early

HUGH BAINBRIDGE WOKE from a half-sleep to the strident hiss and stentorian clank of a steam engine, somewhere close by. Dawn had not yet penetrated the bed of the scrub-clad gully where he and his companions had spent the night, but delicate beams and pin-like golden shafts were dimpling the interlacing network of tree branches and leaves overhead.

'Struth!' Wally Steiler, who had been nodding beside the fire, sat bolt upright, eyes darting. 'That sounded like it was right next to us.'

'Over the spur, I reckon – where that basin should be.' Emil Steiler had zipped up his wind cheater and was reaching for his old shotgun. Within minutes, the fire was doused and all three men were on the move, munching on dried fruit and swigging from water bottles as they went. In short order they were breaking out onto the spur, casting their gaze around through the uncertain light, listening intently to try and pinpoint the train's location and direction of travel.

Down the spur they went, alert for any sound or hint of movement that might reveal an entrance to, or exit from, the mysterious vanishing crater. As the trio closed in toward the rocky knob, the very ground beneath their feet began to pulse and shake; and amidst the mechanical throb of the vast steam engine rising to a crescendo, an old familiar rhythm came drifting through to Hugh's consciousness – the sound of booted feet, marching across a parade ground and pounding aboard railway carriages.

IN THE SEMI-darkness beside one of the compound's demountable buildings, Tessa Scott huddled, watching and waiting, only a few feet from the steam-swirled carriages and freight wagons of the hissing *Diablo*. All night long she had laboured alongside other inmates of the enclosure, helping to attach armour plating, a battering ram, gas tanks and other assorted hardware to the train, reluctantly assisting its conversion into a hulking, terrestrial dreadnought. Then, as dawn broke and the great roof folded back eerily into the crater's upper ledges, the lawyer had at last seized her chance. Amid the clamour and confusion of troops boarding, artillery being loaded, and the locomotive being fuelled and stoked to full pressure, Tess had melted back into the shadows, while her fellow prisoners, their spirits clearly oppressed by weeks of intimidation, milled out mechanically into the open yard.

Tessa's daring ploy paid quick dividends, for amid a sea of khaki uniforms, she soon recognised the slouching figure and sullen demeanour of the guard Herman, shuffling towards her from the train; and someone – it sounded like Inspector Jensen – was barking orders at the man from the closest carriage: 'Bring out that extra bundle o' gas masks, and stash 'em with that other stuff in the rear van: then get in there yourself and be ready to dish the gear out when it's called for.'

'Why yes, your high and bloody mightiness,' the guard muttered *sotto voce*. 'Three bags friggin' full, sir. Why don't ya do some friggin' work yerself, for a change?'

As the reluctant 'quartermaster' cursed and clattered his way into the supply shed next to Tessa, she was struck by the potential opportunity his presence offered. Herman was about her own height, if a little heavier. Getting her own clothes back was always going to be a dicey proposition – for one thing, she could not be sure whether they had been left in the same place, or if they had already been destroyed; at best, they would provide only a marginal camouflage advantage over the orange prisoner garb which she currently wore. The uniform of the embarking enemy, on the other hand, seemed to offer a real chance of avoiding detection. There was, unfortunately, only one way into the shed, through the 'front' entrance taken by Herman – but it was now or never. As the wan sun thrust more and more prying beams over the crater lip, Tessa darted around the corner of the building and through the doorway.

From inside the shed, she could hear a general

hubbub and clamour aboard the train, but no alarm seemed to be directed at her. The overall ambience of deployment – of people concentrating solely on their own tasks, or the activities of those close by – was unchanged. Herman was now directly in front of her, absorbed in gathering bundles of gas masks and shoving them into two hessian bags for easy carrying. She padded up behind him, using all the stealth she could muster, until a loose section of flooring provoked a hideous *creak* and the man spun around, dropping the masks and grabbing for a pistol.

Tessa darted forward, her rigidly extended hand striking deep into the juncture of the guard's neck and shoulder. The man's body jack-knifed and Tess caught his weight just in time to prevent him crashing heavily to the floor. She lowered him down gently and caught her breath.

'Well, no time to be prudish now, old girl,' the lawyer told herself. Quickly she rolled the unconscious figure over, removed his tunic and trousers, and changed into them with almost theatrical speed. She was forced to pull the man's belt in quite a few notches and to quickly abandon any thoughts of donning his size twelve combat boots – instead she would stay with her own hiking shoes, uttering a heart-felt prayer that no one would notice. The transformation was then completed by tucking up her shoulder length brown hair under the guard's floppy hat, and a moment later Tess was sallying forth from the shed, with a hessian bag full of gas masks on either shoulder and her face bent low between them.

'Bout bloody time,' snarled the voice of Inspector Jensen, as she lurched past him through a miasma of coal steam and exquisitely-timed morning mist which now swirled about the train carriages. 'I was just comin' to look for you. Get on board!'

Rather than risking a worded reply, Tessa simply grunted as gutturally as she could, kept moving and clambered awkwardly aboard the van at the back of the train, grateful that Jensen wasn't the type to offer anyone a hand with their load. Once inside the seat-less compartment, she quickly dropped down amongst the masks and other hardware, to await with nail-biting anxiety the moment of departure. She had taken pity on the unconscious Herman by throwing a couple of military blankets over his shorts and singlet clad frame: she had also taken the precaution of tying his hands behind his back with a torn shirt and wrapping a handkerchief around his mouth, though she imagined it would not take him long to wriggle free of both. Her assessment proved correct, for in just under five minutes a ranting, half-naked figure rushed out into the parade ground, to scream out a frenzied alarm that an impostor was aboard the train. Herman's words, however, were swept away in a stream of steam, smoke and coal dust, the frantically rising pitch of his voice drowned out by the hiss and clank of the *Diablo*, powering its way into a newly-revealed tunnel on the lower southern wall of the crater.

'THAR SHE BLOWS!' Hugh Bainbridge, now running ahead of the Steiler brothers towards the peak of Cattle Mountain, turned to look south and east. Having retraced the route of their previous evening's crawl through the thick scrub on the northern edge of the crater, the three men had minutes ago seen the last folds of the 'stadium roof' billow back into the clifftops, had watched the troop-filled train's departure through Hugh's spyglass, and had quickly ruled out any attempt at clambering down the walls, due both to their incredible steepness and the fact that they would be in full view of any guards. Instead, by gaining the summit, they hoped to get a clearer view of the whole mountainside and perhaps see where the *Diablo* would make its exit from the crater – a spot which might in turn provide *them* with an entry point. Thus the professor's exultant shout when a column of smoke suddenly pinpointed the train's position.

As the trio paused and watched, breathless, just above the scrub-shrouded rise which topped the crater, they soon saw the great steaming leviathan come plunging up a lightly forested spur. It was moving more quickly than they thought possible.

'Look at the way that bloody thing weaves between trees,' Wally Steiler gasped in amazement, as the cohorts sought cover behind a lantana thicket. 'And how it hovers just above the ground.'

At close quarters, now perhaps a mere hundred yards from their hide, the train was indeed an awe-inspiring sight – shrieking, hammering, hissing up the slope, while floating almost ethereally on the morning mist. There could be no doubt, however, that this mechanical marvel, loaded to capacity with illegally-sanctioned troops, was solid and all too real, and that its mission was one of menace to legitimate society. The question was: how to stop it?

The three men exchanged bemused glances – should they even try to stop the train? Was it likely that Tess was on board? Or should the priority be to retrace the train's passage, following its route back down the mountainside to the tunnel whence it emerged; from where, using the element of surprise, they might attempt a rescue of all the crater prisoners? As the *Diablo* swept past them and on toward the crest of the ridge, the decision suddenly made itself; for on the platform behind the rear van, three figures – two in khaki uniforms and one in a charcoal suit – could be seen engaged in a desperate struggle.

Chapter Eighteen

TESSA HAD BEEN preparing to escape from the *Diablo's* stores compartment almost from the moment the train had cleared the tunnel and started its ascent of the ridge spur, her idea being simply to wait till they were a prudent distance from the shaft entrance, then to exit via the rear platform and tumble off into the bush. Her plans had been thwarted, however, by the arrival of two powerfully-muscled commando types – both armed with Russian assault rifles – who had entered the van and begun to rummage around for extra clips of ammunition. Burrowing back beneath bags of gas masks and other loose equipment, the girl huddled against the compartment wall, trying to time the sound of her own breathing with the hiss and clatter of the train as it forged on up the hillside.

'Got what I need, cock,' one of the men soon announced, before departing toward the front of the train with the same haste that had characterised his arrival, while the other lingered – frustratingly, infuriatingly – fingering his moustache and rifling through metal containers.

'I want one o' those bayonets I saw earlier,' the man said aloud. 'Now where'd that bloody Herman put 'em? Come to think of it, where is that idiot? Out on the back platform?'

Tessa tensed her muscles, crouching like a panther preparing to launch itself from cover, every faculty keyed and focused on the man before her. And then Inspector Jensen charged into the carriage, waving a walkie-talkie around and shouting like a man possessed.

'Herman's just been on the bloody blower. That smart alec legal eagle bitch has got away – decked him and took his uniform! She's prob'ly still on the train – under our noses! Quick, ya clown; start chuckin' that gear aside and see if she's hidden behind it, or under it.'

Both men plunged forward, arms flailing and hands groping furiously. Gas masks, tins and water bottles began to erupt in all directions, a process dramatically accelerated as Tessa suddenly exploded out from the piles of stores and equipment and flew between the men, on a beeline for the rear door. Both assailants grabbed at her but she darted swiftly beneath their clutches, fending Jensen off with a straight arm jab and tripping the commando up with a kick to the ankle. In a flash she was out on the platform and preparing to swing up over the safety rail, but the fast moving commando was right behind her, seizing the girl in a bear-like embrace which clamped her arms to her sides. As the mercenary dragged Tessa away from the railing, she came face to face with Jensen, who emerged from the van with a malicious smirk.

'Righto, Trixie Belden!' The dark-suited inspector lurched forward, raising a hairy fist. 'How'd you like a smack on that turned-up toffee nose? Smart arse silvertail lawyers; you're all the bloody same.'

Tessa leaned her weight back against the commando's upper body, swung up her long legs and drove both feet straight into the approaching policeman's chest. As Jensen staggered back against the carriage door, she allowed herself to go limp in the soldier's grasp, then looped her foot back around his ankle and twisted, once more throwing him off balance. She drove an elbow back into the man's middle, succeeded in breaking his grip, then caught his flailing right arm with both hands and rolled forward, using her opponent's considerable weight and momentum to propel him over her shoulder. As the commando struck the floor with a crash, Tess vaulted over the platform railing, hitting the ground running – first in the same direction as the train, then darting off toward the nearest thicket of scrub.

The lawyer crouched low as she ran, trying to blend her khaki uniform into clumps of long grass and shrubbery, but it was soon clear that her escape was being closely monitored, for spurts of dirt began to kick up on either side of her zig-zag course. A small branch was sheared off a sapling within inches of her head and as she rapidly switched direction another bullet keened off a granite outcrop just ahead. Then, in answer to the staccato bark of the Kalashnikov behind came the crack of two long-barrelled hunting rifles from off to one side. Tessa dropped down into the grass, unable to restrain a wild laugh of exultation: Hugh and Wally were returning the mercenary's fire, and though both shots were deliberately aimed high above the door of the rear carriage, they provided sufficient incentive to send both the commando and the corrupt police officer scurrying back inside. In an instant Hugh had sprinted to meet Tessa, arms outstretched, and the girl's face had buried itself against his chest.

'Dear, dear Miss Muffet,' he said softly. 'For heaven's sake, say you're all right. Goodness me; we've run across a rough bunch this time. If they've harmed you, I swear – '

'It's all right, darling,' she murmured gently. 'I'm fine. But we must talk quickly – and act quickly. That train has got the equivalent of chemical weapons on board: somehow, some way, it must be stopped.'

Wally and Emil now joined the pair, their united gaze lifting toward the upper slopes and the horn of Cattle Mountain. The *Diablo* was already cresting the range saddle, to begin its slow yet inexorable descent into the next valley.

'It's heading overland for Warumbah,' Tess explained quickly. 'Their plan is to kidnap the Prime Minister, who's arriving there for a conference today, along with two state Premiers. They've got a methane concoction on board, which will cause a lot of discomfort in the streets, but they've also got sarin nerve gas and they'll use it at the slightest sign of resistance. The train carriages are armour-plated and they're bristling with armed commando types – mercenaries and what-not – all in khaki, like me.'

'So it's an insurrection – an attempt to overthrow the elected government?' Hugh's face registered his amazement.

'Exactly. Or, as they see it, more of a corporate takeover. The ringleaders are Maurice Arblaster, the creator – or Frankenstein – of the *Diablo*, and Jemima Blackman, whose company chemists have created the toxic payload. Oh, and of course, that obnoxious police inspector – Jensen.'

'What's their troop strength, do you think?' Fully reassured of Tessa's well-being, Hugh was now leading his three companions at a brisk jog-trot up the mountain spur.

'Seventy to eighty, at the minimum,' the lawyer estimated. 'Possibly a hundred or more. It was hard to tell in the half-light just how many pairs of booted feet were going in and out of those carriages.'

'Hmm. Sounds like good odds.' Despite the morning chill, the professor was mopping his brow as they crested the razor-back ridge, some two hundred yards south of the mountain peak. Their newly-attained vantage point soon revealed the *Diablo* and its caravan, winding to and fro between the greenery, like some malevolent steaming caterpillar crawling its way down the western slope of the range. Responding almost automatically, the four companions started down in pursuit, until the whine of bullets off an adjacent rock face and the ensuing sounds of gunfire sent them plunging into the cover of a brushy gully. Those had been very near misses, clearly too close to be intended as warning shots, making it obvious that the squad on board the train were covering their rear flank with field glasses and telescopic sights.

'Somehow I think we've got to pull back,' Hugh whistled. 'Get to a phone, if we can, and try to contact the legitimate authorities. I know we've still got the problem of knowing whom to trust, but I'm wondering if we could somehow get through to the PM, or his people. Perhaps the security services – ASIO, are they called? – or the Commonwealth Police; maybe the armed forces? Surely, they can't have moles everywhere.'

Tessa's face wore a worried frown. 'The problem we then have, of course, is the safety of the hostages back in the crater. From what I learned back there, the minute their progress is baulked or resisted by authorities, someone – Jemima particularly – will order the compound to be pumped with sarin nerve gas. She seems to be itching to do it.'

'Struth!' Emil gasped in amazement. 'She must be a real cow of a thing, that one.'

'The other constraint is that of time,' Tess explained. 'This end of the valley is sparsely populated. To get to a phone where we knew we were welcome, and safe, we'd have to run back to Wally and Emil's place, or one of their trusted near neighbours. Once that train gets down onto the valley floor, it only has to travel up and over a couple more ridges and then it's up on the Darling Downs. It could be in Warumbah in – well – probably inside forty minutes. It's going to be a close run thing.'

'Unless...' Hugh was peering upward, his gaze apparently fixed on the summit of Cattle Mountain. For a moment, he appeared to be lost in thought.

'Unless what?' Tessa prompted.

'Tell me, Wally,' said the professor almost airily. 'Do you reckon you could hit the base of that boulder – the one almost on top of Cattle Mountain?'

'Reckon I could, yeah.' Wally shouldered his .250/3000, letting the scope crosshairs settle on the narrow neck of granite and loose stones which appeared to hold the vast rock in position near the peak.

'You recall, Muffet, when we had lunch up on the summit, how we both remarked on the precarious toehold of that granite boulder, and its potential to go tumbling off down the mountainside some day?' As Tessa murmured assent, Hugh shifted his gaze back to the mountain top. 'The thing is, which way is it most likely to roll?'

'Down that spur, beyond the next gully,' Wally opined. 'That'd be my guess.'

'And mine,' said Tessa.

Emil was peering hard down into the valley. 'An' that train's gonna cross that spur further down shortly, snakin' this way and that across the slope the way it's doin'. By heck, it just might work – might stuff up their runnin' gear, their hoverin' system, or somethin'.'

'It's worth a try, don't you think?' Hugh said, raising his own rifle. 'If we can somehow delay them, put them out of action at least temporarily, perhaps we can then get to a phone and warn the proper authorities.'

The crack of the professor's .275 Rigby now echoed across the hillside, and through his Bushnell 6 power scope Wally Steiler saw a shard of stone and a puff of powdered granite fly from the base of the boulder. The bushman then squeezed the trigger of his own rifle, and was rewarded by a second eruption of rock chips and dust from the ledge. He also noticed the big boulder gyrate slightly, before settling down again on its bed of lesser stones.

'Course if that rock does happen to come rollin' this way,' Emil observed sagely, 'we'd all better be ready to start sprintin'.'

'Given that scenario, I believe I could almost

knock Ovett out of the next Olympics squad,' Hugh said, aiming carefully and firing again. This time the neck of granite at the base appeared to completely dissolve and the boulder tipped forward dramatically; yet once again it stabilised, frustratingly lodged on its mountainside supports. A downward glance revealed the *Diablo* nosing its way onto and across the spur, inexorably pursuing its zig zag course down to the valley floor, from which point its deadly mission would be a *fait accompli*.

Wally Steiler ejected a fired cartridge case, caught it and fed a new round into the chamber of his rifle. 'You know, I reckon I can see what's holdin' the bloody thing up,' he said positively, before again lowering his cheek onto the Savage Model 20's stock. An instant later, the rifle barked and a house-brick sized rock, which appeared to be acting as a pivot beneath the larger boulder, was split asunder. Once more the monster lurched forward – only to pause, maddeningly, on the very lip of the ledge.

'Bloody hell!' roared Wally.

'It looks like it's been caught up on a mere pebble.' Hugh lowered his iron-sighted rifle and trained his brass telescope on the peak. 'A confounded stone that would fit inside the palm of your hand.'

'We'll see about that.' Again came the stentorian crack of the .250/3000, and suddenly all hell broke loose. The vast monolith came bounding forth, barrelling and bouncing down the mountainside, gathering up a constellation of rocks, saplings and lesser missiles as it went, filling the valley with a thunderous swelling roar.

'Well done, that man!' Hugh shouted above the din.

The driver of the *Diablo* must have seen the approaching avalanche because the train appeared to levitate and turn sharply almost at the same instant. The man's idea had clearly been to quickly elevate the loco and carriages above most of the rocks and debris and also to turn downhill out of the slide's path, but the sudden manoeuvre seemed to de-stabilise the train, for it listed over on its axis away from the slope. It was then that the giant boulder, rebounding like a beach ball off a small plateau on the spur, struck the tank of the mighty steam engine, and the *Diablo*'s destiny was sealed. Mortally hit, the vast steaming locomotive heeled over even further, to a point where gravity dealt the final blow. For a moment, the *Diablo*'s carriages seemed to be fighting to keep it upright, but the engine's gigantic weight, coupled with the already canted attitude of the entire train, eventually brought the complete serpentine structure over. Coiling and writhing, the train pitched onto its side, some of the carriages sliding several yards down the spur and gully wall, before coming to rest with roofs angled toward the valley.

'Well, it looks like we stopped the bugger,' Emil Steiler commented dryly. 'An' now the trouble's really gonna start. Those blokes look as mad as hornets.'

A glance down the hillside quickly confirmed Emil's observation, for squads of khaki-clad troops were now hatching like larvae from the body of the *Diablo*. Within seconds they were forming into ranks in the nearest gully, responding in trained fashion to the bellowed commands of Maurice Arblaster, whose hulking, dark-suited figure had emerged from the locomotive with a megaphone. Several other people, including a man and a woman in fashionable town dress, and another male in jeans and bush gear, darted out of the front carriage, then drifted off into the scrub – Jensen and Jemima almost certainly, with a local ally acting as guide. But it was the bear-like businessman with his loud-hailer who arrested Hugh's attention.

'We need that thing,' the professor said decisively, a statement which prompted curious looks from his colleagues.

'What did you have in mind, Hugh?' Tess inquired. 'We're horribly outnumbered.'

'We'll have to convince them otherwise,' Hugh replied. 'It strikes me that these fellows down below won't know the country all that well. They probably haven't been here in the district long enough. Now if we could succeed in keeping to the scrubby gullies, and fan out around them, perhaps we could get across the idea that the cavalry has arrived, so to speak. A few shouted commands; some frequent, judicious shifts in our positions; a few shots from different angles – it might just do the trick, what? But I'd like to get hold of that megaphone.'

'All right then: let's give it a whirl,' Wally suggested, melting off into the thickets of an overgrown gully to their left.

The commandos were now fanning out across the spur, ascending in three serried lines up the mountainside toward the spot where they had last sighted their annoyers. Behind them, on a rock outcrop not far from the wreck of his train, sat a red-faced, sweating Arblaster, urging them on through his megaphone.

'Garn – get up that hill, you mob. That's what you're bein' paid for. Find the perpetrators of this, and I'll double your money. We're still in business, don't worry. This is a minor setback – there'll be a new *Diablo* if necessary. We've got a hole in the mountain and a roof to conceal it when we need to; workshops and miles o' tunnels. Just find 'em. It's that pommy bastard professor behind this, and so help me I want his hide.'

'Hmm. I get the impression he probably likes you deep down.' Tessa shot Hugh an amused grimace. 'He just doesn't know you that well.'

'A situation I'll soon be pleased to rectify,' the

professor quipped back. The pair were now forging down a narrow, thickly-covered ravine which cut down the mountain slope alongside the largely clear spur being climbed by the commandos. On the opposite side of this spur ran the scrubby gully selected for cover by Wally. Emil Steiler, meanwhile, had back-tracked uphill a short distance, then moved slightly north across the mountain slope, where he ensconced himself in a stand of thick timber, above and to the left of the approaching squad.

Tessa and Hugh soon checked their downhill dash and sank low into the available cover while the mercenaries pounded past above them. Stealthily moving off again, they quickly pin-pointed Arblaster's position, for the engineer-magnate was once more ranting on his loud hailer.

'Push on. Find every one of 'em – there can't be many – and bring their carcases back 'ere. There'll be no worries as long as word doesn't get out; and they're the only ones who can get it out. We'll soon rebuild – we got plenty o' finance, and plenty o' support across the business sector. Just find those bastards and we can move on.'

As the tirade rose to a crescendo and sank at last to a hoarse whisper, Hugh and Tessa peeped up from the ravine to see Arblaster, apparently alone on his stony perch, setting down his megaphone on a nearby rock and pulling out a hip flask from a coat pocket. His gorilla-like form was clad in an expensive suit – no doubt in anticipation of television appearances announcing another successful takeover – but the overall picture was of a man completely out of control, consumed by seething rage and frustration. His face was livid as he rose to his feet, pulled savagely at the flask, then cast his gaze around for his major co-conspirators.

'Where's that bloody Jemima, and Jensen?' he grunted. 'They both got out o' the wreck all right. Everybody did. They must know where I am. The thing was only goin' slow when it tipped over, so I don't reckon anyone took hardly a scratch. So where have they got – ?'

This bizarre soliloquy, true in its basic assumptions, was suddenly interrupted by a polite 'Good morning', as out of the scrub came someone Arblaster clearly did not expect to see.

'You – ' the businessman almost shrieked. 'You jumped-up, pointy-headed, academic bastard – I hate you and all your kind.'

'Ah, sirrah,' rejoined the professor. 'Well met then.'

'And you come walkin' out here, bold as brass. I got a hundred men out lookin' for you.'

Hugh nodded sagely. '*They seek him here, they seek him there*, one supposes.'

'Why you- I'll kill ya meself!' So saying, the enraged giant plucked up a chunk of granite from the nearby outcrop, swung it overhead and rushed at the professor.

'Hugh, look out!' Tessa yelled, as Arblaster abruptly truncated his charge and launched the rock straight at the professor's head. Bainbridge side-stepped adroitly and, as the rock went crashing past into the shrubbery, prepared himself to meet the troll-like figure's second assault. This time the weapon was a three metre long sapling, which Arblaster had uprooted and was now wielding like a lance.

'Talk about a scenery-chewing performance.' The professor shook his head in apparent disbelief, then darted forward, ducking and weaving as Westmead had taught him to do when facing a bulkier opponent. As Arblaster attempted to alter the direction of his charge to meet the constantly switching angle of Hugh's approach, he overbalanced and the don seized the advantage, landing a hard left on the hulking figure's chin and a right hook to follow through. Arblaster dropped the sapling and staggered backwards, clutching at a low branch for support and then tearing it down to swipe at Hugh's head. The professor swept up a short lump of fallen timber in time to block the giant's blow, but he had clearly had enough of the man's refusal to fight cleanly. Darting behind Arblaster, Hugh simply clobbered him on the head with the wood, turning to Tessa almost apologetically as the magnate sprawled unconscious to the ground.

'I'm not sure if the estimable Westmead would

have entirely approved of that last manoeuvre,' he explained. 'But two can play at these batting games. And anyway, it saved time.'

Chapter Nineteen

THE COMMANDO SQUAD had reached a lightly-timbered plateau at the top of the spur and were casting their gaze in all directions for the wreckers of their train. Above them, leading up to the ridge crest, were steeply-angled grassy slopes, criss-crossed by wallaby trails and peppered here and there with ironbarks, grass trees and occasional stands of thicker cover. In one of these coverts sat Emil Steiler, cradling his old 12 bore and waiting for a signal from Hugh.

On the southern side of the commandos was the head of the scrub-choked gully where Wally had his stand, while the opposite side of the spur fell down into the ravine which Hugh and Tessa had used to get down to Arblaster. Having tied that worthy up with scrub vines and gagged him with a handkerchief, the pair now worked their way back up the ravine until they were a little under two hundred yards below the mercenaries' position. Crawling up into a lantana thicket, which though uncomfortable provided both excellent cover and a clear view of the soldiers, the couple quickly confirmed their strategy, with Tessa taking over the rifle and Hugh the loud hailer.

'Before I make my announcement, Muffet, can you plonk a shot right above their heads?' As he spoke, Hugh was observing the uniformed men on the plateau through his brass telescope. 'Perhaps they're not as good a fighting unit as they think they are, for the place they've chosen to stop doesn't have a lot of cover. Either that, or they're an arrogant lot and they don't take us seriously. Anyway, let's see if we can give them a jolt.'

'Let's. And the minute I fire, it's certain that Wally and Emil will follow suit. *One for all, and all for one*, eh?' Tess shot Hugh a radiant smile before lowering her face onto the rifle stock. An instant later, there was a thunderous crack, followed by a chorus of confused yells from the commandos as a low branch, sheared off an ironbark tree by the .275's 160 grain bullet, fell right in the middle of the huddled group.

'A Squad, move in!' Hugh bellowed through the megaphone, and in response a slug from Wally Steiler's rifle tore up the dirt between one of the commando's feet. The confusion multiplied as the boom of Emil Steiler's old single-barrel shotgun echoed across the slopes, and a shower of falling pellets and gum tree twigs rained down on the soldiers, sending them milling in all directions for the scant cover available.

'B Squad, close in!' shouted Hugh, as Tessa smoothly worked the Rigby's bolt and sent another shot up the slope, tearing a sapling out of a thicket which one of the commandos was just about to enter. The man hurriedly changed his mind and scrambled up the slope in a different direction, while the professor issued another proclamation through the loud speaker: 'This is Commander Allan Somerville of the Australian Commonwealth Police. Those were warning shots – deliberately aimed high or low. You are completely surrounded, and you are all under arrest as an unauthorised and illegal militia. Throw down your arms and walk out into the clear part of the plateau, with your hands above your heads. I repeat; you are *completely* surrounded.'

For a moment it was touch and go. A couple of the more hardened mercenaries seemed prepared to argue the toss. 'This is bullshit,' came a broad South African accent. 'There cawn't be many of them, police or no police. We can still fight our way out.' The sun-burnt figure brandished an AK-47 high in the air as encouragement to his colleagues.

'Y'all heard the man.' A voice from the Carolinas drifted down the mountain. 'Let's give them federal suckers a run for their money.'

Their reply was another blast from Emil's shotgun, which peppered the branches overhead – except this time it came not from above, but from a thick clump of scrub close by on their right flank. Seconds later, Wally's rifle sounded again, also from a new direction, and the Kalashnikov rifle was torn from the Afrikaner's grasp, to lie a mangled wreck on the ground. Adding further to the confusion – not just of the commandos but of those opposing them – there now came another shot, from further up the slope. It was a dull, flat report, which none of the four friends recognised, but the bullet fell near the American mercenary's feet and was clearly intended to further intimidate the commandos.

'Someone else joining the resistance, Muffet?' Hugh and Tessa exchanged surprised glances.

'All contributions gratefully received,' quipped the lawyer. 'The more the merrier at the moment.'

The recent multi-directional fusillade was the straw that broke the camel's back for the commando squad. As Hugh had begun to suspect, many of their number were not seasoned veterans or well-trained mercenaries at all, but rather disgruntled misfits looking for a cause or, in some cases, street punks just looking for the next big brawl. Rabble or not, however, they were still a dangerous mob, and it was a glad sight for Hugh, Tessa and the Steiler brothers when row upon row of uniformed men first began to walk out into the open with their hands empty and high in the air. The four colleagues now closed in, cautiously circling the little plateau while keeping themselves within range of cover.

For Hugh, as the one member of the party with any military experience, the most urgent need was to somehow maintain the facade of strength. Once the commandos realised they had been tricked, it seemed probable that the situation would again become volatile. It was thus important, the professor believed, to swiftly pinpoint and isolate any 'hard men' in particular, and get them secured with vines, strips of clothing or anything else that might be at hand. He had resolved to start calling a few obvious candidates forward – for it was clearly out of the question to go in amongst the mob – when a cacophony of cooees and yells came drifting up the slope.

A small band of valley and hill farmers, several of whom were recognised by the Steilers as near neighbours, could now be seen trekking up the spur. Clearly, they had heard the crash of the *Diablo* and the ensuing melee, and had come to investigate. The obvious question that had to be answered was whether they were friend or foe. Some of the newcomers were armed, but by their open approach, their effusive greetings, and their ready acceptance of Wally's explanations, it was soon apparent that none of the new arrivals belonged to Inspector Jensen's local intelligence network. They were soon participating enthusiastically in the commandos' capture, gathering up weaponry, tying up sullen prisoners and standing guard. At this point, however, with less than a dozen people attempting to control almost a hundred, it was obvious that something could still easily go awry – and it did!

The South African mercenary, at Hugh's suggestion one of the first to be tied up, had for several minutes been chafing his less-experienced cohorts for their apparent lack of backbone and their failure to make a quick rush at their captors. 'These awn't coppers anymore than I am,' he snarled. 'They've pulled a smart trick on us, but they cawn't arrest yew. What awe you – men or mice? Attack 'em, yew pansies.'

'But I *am* a copper,' oozed a new voice from the sidelines. 'And I *can* arrest people.' Accompanied by a red-faced man in elastic-sided boots and other bushman's kit, a dark-suited Inspector Jensen stepped forth from the scrub, with a pistol trained on Hugh's head.

'OK then; I could arrest this toffee-nosed pom and his smart alec girlfriend right now but, unless you lot drop your guns, I reckon I'll just waste 'em – solve a few problems straight off.'

'You harm either one of 'em,' said Wally Steiler evenly. 'An' I'll drop you in your tracks.' For one excruciating moment it was a classic stand-off, a situation which seemed just as likely to go either way.

'There won't be any need for that, Mr Steiler.' A new voice – youthful yet strangely crisp and confident – suddenly floated down into the suspense-filled amphitheatre from the rocks above. 'Although I can't say I blame you. I'm also a policeman, however, and I too can arrest people. I'm arresting you now, Inspector Jensen – you, and the whole bang lot of these toy soldiers in uniform.'

Constable Ben Baker, his service revolver

trained unwaveringly on Jensen, jumped down onto the plateau, took several quick strides across to the inspector, and disarmed him. If Jensen had thought quickly enough, he might well have counter-bluffed or resisted, but he relied instead on bombast, even as the young constable slapped handcuffs on him.

'Come on, Baker; ya don't turn in your own. You don't rat on your mates, you scum.'

'No, Inspector, *you're* the scum,' Ben Baker said tersely. 'And it's mongrels like you who give the whole force – the other 99.9 per cent anyway – a bad name.'

The constable now turned toward Tessa, Hugh, the Steilers and the neighbours who had joined them.

'Righto then: I'm now authorising you people – after the fact I s'pose – to make citizen's arrests and to hold these commandos, at gunpoint if necessary. Some people might say you've acted like vigilantes, but in a case like this I reckon you had no choice. You wouldn't have known who to trust. Neither did I. Some of my superior officers are as bent as Uri Geller's fork, and it appears that some of the locals around here have been acting as agents and informants for them.' He jerked a thumb meaningly at the man who had accompanied – indeed guided – Inspector Jensen away from the train and up through the gully in order to spring his surprise.

'Yeah, well that's ol' Ned Schwartz from West Hatton,' said Emil Steiler gruffly. 'Shout him a few bottles o' rum and he's your friend for life.'

'Well, he won't get much of it inside the clink,' said the constable. 'What I'm really sorry about is how long it's taken me to figure this whole thing out. After this Jensen, with all his cohorts, arrived in town, with all sorts of official lookin' paperwork supposedly from CIB; well, they just took over – or should I say "shut down" – any investigation to do with missing persons or sightings of the train. Very handy, because the train was being used, so I gather, to abduct people, who have since been used as slave labour in that crater across the ridge. I don't mind telling you people that I wasn't too sure about you lot either for a while. I'd been keeping an eye on that old dairy across the mountain, based on a few rumours I'd heard around the place, and ever since I saw some of you there yesterday afternoon, I've been shadowing you. It wasn't easy, I might say – especially sitting out on the spur last night without a fire, while you blokes were down in the gully warming yourselves.'

'Our apologies for that,' Hugh said. 'If we'd only known – still, we're enormously grateful that you did follow us, *and* for what you've done since; particularly as these chaps were starting to look like a handful. I don't wish to embarrass you, constable, but let me just say that you're an exemplar for your profession.'

'Yeah; you did a bloody good job, mate.' Wally Steiler slapped the slightly red-faced constable on the shoulder.

'The funny thing is; the whole time I was following you, I was debating whether to arrest you, or to call the case in. But, as I said before, I didn't know who to trust. Now it strikes me that we've still got a pretty volatile situation here. The safest way, I think, is to call in the army and the federal authorities, because this is really like an insurrection I suppose. I've got a police radio in the car. Oh, and by the way – Professor Bainbridge, isn't it?'

'Yes,' Hugh smiled.

'I'm not sure how to tell you this, but there's actually no such thing as a commander in the Australian Commonwealth Police.'

'Oh well, you can't win 'em all.' The professor laughed aloud. 'I'm glad none of those blighters picked up on it.'

'Call me cautious, constable,' Tessa said. 'But I'm wondering if it might just be prudent to call in the Commonwealth authorities from a private phone, rather than via your walkie-talkie or police radio. As you've pointed out, we still don't know whom to trust, and back in the crater there are still a group of prisoners – potential hostages – to be considered. We'll also have to notify emergency services, in case the gas tanks aboard that train have ruptured.'

'We can ring from my place,' one of the farmers

suggested. 'My house is only half a mile or so away.'

'Gas tanks?' The constable looked at Tessa in astonishment.

'Yes – holding toxic gas. Mind you, they are triple-reinforced containers, inside armoured carriages and, if any does escape, it should dissipate fairly quickly out in open or tree-clad countryside; but nonetheless, it is sarin nerve gas and it will have to be dealt with by experts. And that reminds me; where is the perpetrator of this gas outrage? I'm sure I saw her come out of the train wreck and run off into the scrub, so she shouldn't have any radio contact with base. But still …'

Behind them came a loud guffaw from Inspector Jensen. 'Good luck with catchin' her. She's already on her way back to the compound, and I can tell you she means business.'

'What are you talking about – "she means business"?' Tessa rounded on the man.

Again the bent copper laughed. 'Well, after we got out o' the train, she came up the gully with me an' that yokel Schwartz. We decided between us that in case my stunt here didn't work, there should be a back-up – a plan B, you know. We'd lost radio contact in the crash, so old Mima's presently leggin' it back over the mountain to the compound – even as we speak, she's hot-footin' it there. I don't need to tell you that we've got hostages back in that crater. – quite a few of 'em; plus we've got old Herman and a few idiot guards who'll back us up. I reckon we'll negotiate a deal yet – safe passage out o' the country, an' maybe a few mill in cash besides. O' course, the mood old Mima's in, I reckon she's gonna throw on a demonstration o' that sarin gas the minute she gets there – try it out on a few o' those hostages, you know, just to show the powers-that-be that we mean business. A few o' the guards might go west too o' course, but – ah – what's the odds? "Retribution", she called it, for the wreck o' the *Diablo*.'

Tessa's face was strained but determined as she turned back to her colleagues. 'Hugh, I'm going to cut across the ridge and try to overtake her,' she said with a supreme attempt at calmness. 'I think you and Wally and Emil will have to assist Constable Baker in keeping order here.' As if to forestall any possible argument, she began to turn away.

'Muffet,' said Hugh softly. Tess glanced back toward him.

'Do be careful,' he smiled.

Her eyes thanked him, before she spun on her heel and bounded off up the slope.

'Lots o' luck, Trixie Belden,' the sneering voice of Inspector Jensen echoed up from the plateau behind her. 'She's got five minutes head start, an' she runs like the wind. An' she's one tough little piece o' North Shore fluff.'

A couple of thoughts gave Tessa cause for optimism as she ran. For one thing, there was her outfit. That hastily-borrowed khaki combat uniform might not be a fashion statement but it did allow considerable freedom of movement. By contrast, Jemima had appeared to be clad in glamorously elegant, yet undoubtedly restrictive, designer daywear; probably with unforgiving dress shoes, for like Arblaster, and to a lesser extent Jensen, the ringleaders had all clearly been expecting to announce their *coup d'etat* on national television.

Another potential advantage was the length of her own stride: while Tessa did not rate herself as a fantastic sprinter, she knew she could cover ground swiftly, particularly along bush tracks. This led on to the issue of local knowledge, and a short-cut which the lawyer hoped desperately that Jemima would not know. From the previous afternoon's episode it was obvious that the business-woman *did* know her way up and down at least one of the spurs which ran past the crater and on up to the ridge crest, but Tessa herself had almost forgotten about the 'hidden gorge' – a twisted ravine which cut straight through the saddle, some two hundred metres south of Cattle Mountain peak. She had glimpsed the tangle of boulders which hid the rocky chasm's entrance on the first day of this trip to Queensland, when Frank Richards' painting had brought her up here. She had seen those rocks again when cresting the ridge with Hugh and the Steiler brothers yesterday afternoon, and now memories of exploring the cutting, with her own brother and her father, came flooding back from years before. Within seconds, she was in the gorge once more, scrambling upward over slippery shale, through a narrow rock-walled tunnel carved out by centuries of coursing spring water and ridge run-off.

A moment later, Tessa was out in the open – out on the eastern slopes of the ridge, and ready to descend the spur which, further down, flanked the southern side of the crater.

And ahead? *Yes* – surely that *was* Jemima! A flying mane of blonde hair, a silk patterned blouse and business skirt – it was her all right, and now a mere seventy or eighty yards separated them. But the woman was racing like a cheetah down the slope – in low heels, damn it – having apparently jettisoned jacket and scarf somewhere along the track. Ms Blackman was clearly not going to be easy to catch.

Tessa took a deep breath and broke into a long loping stride. Some three hundred and fifty yards down the spur lay the mouth of the tunnel which the *Diablo* had used to exit the crater. For a moment it seemed just conceivable that the businesswoman could be overhauled before reaching it, but as always Jemima was to prove a ferocious competitor. A quick backward glance soon told her that she was being pursued, whereupon her already prodigious pace accelerated still further. While Tessa succeeded in halving the gap between them, the flying mogul tore into the dank passage several seconds ahead. And it took less than half a second, the lawyer told herself as she pounded through the darkness, to throw a lethal switch.

Out into the light of the crater they came, with Jemima powering straight for a yawning hole at the base of the eastern wall. From what Tessa had seen and heard in the past twelve hours, this was clearly the entrance to a shaft giving access to a labyrinth of inter-connecting mine tunnels, the home of the underground railway plied in recent days and weeks by the *Diablo*.

It was obviously also the location of Jemima's gas storage facilities, and no doubt there would be efficient switch gear there which could release the deadly vapours upward, via pipes or hoses, into the compound. But how to stop it happening? Try as she might, Tessa could not close the gap in time!

Suddenly there was a loud crack, which echoed and re-echoed around the compound. Jemima pitched forward, and rolled across the floor of the crater. Tessa ducked behind a boulder, unsure of where the shot had come from. In a moment the source was revealed, along with the actual target.

Angie's boyfriend Warren Schultz had a rifle in his hands, and from a position behind one of the compound walls, the lad seemed to have two guards pinned down behind some scant cover, high on the crater's upper slopes. To one side of young Schultz sat a forlorn Herman, his arms pinioned by the schoolteacher Wesley Smythe and another orange-suited figure.

From the shelter of some boulders just beyond the compound, another guard now returned Warren's fire, but it was soon obvious, to both Tessa and Jemima, that no one was shooting at them. Clearly a spirited resistance had broken out in the basin, and the outcome looked difficult to predict. Perhaps the sound of the train crash and subsequent gunfire had drifted across the mountain to the prisoners, prompting them to launch a do-or-die attack of their own. Or perhaps they had simply seized the opportunity afforded by the relative scarcity of guards and total absence of commandos. The one certainty was that it would all be in vain if Jemima were to reach her lethal switchgear down in the tunnel; and by the look on her face as she rose now to her feet, this would once again be her objective.

Tessa leapt upright and rushed straight for the businesswoman, who just as quickly resumed her sprint for the pit. A flying tackle by the lawyer brought them both down in a tangle of arms and legs, and a moment later they were rolling down the shaft, past the glistening lines of a railway track, over grimy seams of coal and down onto a wood-planked floor between rows of reinforced steel vats.

Surprisingly, there was light everywhere in the tunnel, with blazing electric lamps delineating rows of switches, and glinting off stopcocks attached to metal tubing which ran upward into the cavern roof. The light also revealed a small motorised trolley, undoubtedly intended as an escape vehicle for it was pointed back into the tunnel and equipped with several gas masks.

Fighting like a demon, Jemima bunched up both legs and kicked free of Tessa's grasp, then sprang to her feet and lunged furiously for a brass knob on a pipe beside one of the vats. Just as the blonde woman's hand closed on the gas release however, Tessa seized her arms and forcefully wrenched her away.

Her face a study in rage and frustration, Jemima drove back viciously with her elbow, eliciting a gasp from Tessa and breaking her grip. Spinning on her polished heel, the business mogul swung a punch to Tessa's jaw, sending her reeling backwards with arms flailing. With her hand extended in karate style, Tessa retaliated by chopping hard at her opponent's neck but Jemima somehow swayed back on her feet out of harm's way, and landed another punch which sent the lawyer sprawling over backwards.

'Reckon that's fixed you, dearie!' With an icy smile, Jemima returned to her task, twisting the round brass knob all the way, then ducking just in time to avoid a forged metal rod sweeping in the general direction of her head.

'You little cow!' Jemima turned now to face Angela Reimann, as the young girl, her face crimson with anger and exertion, tried again to heft and swing the iron bar. A kick from the business-woman drove Angie backward and off balance; she dropped the bar but gamely she stood her ground and tried to shape up to her skilled antagonist.

'Angie!' Tessa yelled as she sprang back on her feet and rushed again at Jemima. 'Don't try to fight her. Go for the stopcock. Turn it off – it's pumping poison gas into the crater.'

'You'll never stop me, either of you.' With blonde hair flying about her face, Ms Blackman raced to meet Tessa, who this time skilfully read her opponent's moves and adroitly fended aside her flailing fists. Tessa landed a right cross squarely on the woman's cheek, following up with a straight left to the point of her chin. Jemima staggered away, but recovered enough to bend quickly, scoop up the iron bar and lash out furiously with it. Tess ducked athletically to one side, however, and as the weight of Jemima's weapon dragged her off balance, the lawyer delivered a superb right hook to the businesswoman's jaw. Jemima pitched over backwards onto the floor, and stayed there.

'We'll stop you all right,' Tessa said evenly, before turning to exchange a smile full of pure relief with Angela Reimann, who now stood beaming beside the gas vats.

'I turned it all the way back,' Angie said proudly, pointing to the knob Jemima had used.' It says "off'. I can't turn it any further.'

'You've done it, kiddo,' Tess reassured her. 'I doubt that much of it escaped, and provided it is just a small release it should dissipate pretty quickly in the open air. All the same, I think we should evacuate the area as quickly as possible. If I can just get hold of a loudspeaker, I might be able to persuade those guards that the game is up – oh, and we'll need to secure madam here, I suppose.'

'No worries.' Angela extracted a length of pulley rope from a pile of tunnel maintenance equipment in a nearby corner, rolled the unconscious Jemima over and tied her wrists behind her back. She then followed Tessa up the entrance shaft, staying close to the lawyer as she darted out into the crater and made a beeline for the main administration building. As hoped, they found a loud hailer inside, and in short order the two young women had joined the resistance behind the cover of the compound wall, where Tessa made an announcement which evoked a chorus of cheers from every orange-suited figure in the vicinity.

'The *Diablo* operation is over. You guards have no choice but to surrender. The Commonwealth Police have your leaders and their entire mercenary force in custody, and the Australian Defence forces have been alerted. Your only option is to lay down your arms, and come out now with your hands up.' While Tessa would have given much to check the slight quaver of emotion in her voice while she issued this ultimatum, the effect on her audience soon proved entirely positive. Two khaki-clad men, with hands raised above their heads, soon emerged from behind rocks high up on the basin's western wall, while a third came marching sullenly out of a stores building on the crater floor. The unwilling passengers of the *Diablo* were free at last.

Chapter Twenty

FOR THE NEWLY-LIBERATED prisoners of the crater, the journey out onto the spur and back up over the ridge was a clear triumph of ascendant emotion over physical difficulty. Relief, anticipation, pure joy and exhilaration lent spring to every step, and even the most senior members of the party – farmer Arnie Scheiwe and Angie Riemann's parents – were soon forging across the crest and down the western scarps toward the wreck of the *Diablo*. A heady mixture of camaraderie, hope and wild abandon had quickly transformed the group, and whether one had been a captive for months or for days did not seem to matter – it was just astonishing, and madly elating, to be free. Free again to see the wider world – the trees and pastures, the ploughed ground and distant homesteads – and to breathe again the fresh air, far beyond that pit of iniquity back in the eastern slopes.

But there were still practical tasks to be accomplished. Fully securing the commando mob had proved to be a frustratingly slow, tedious and potentially hazardous process. There were still truculent and uncooperative elements within the mercenary ranks and several times the threat of a mass breakout seemed imminent, so it was with considerable relief that Hugh, Ben Baker and their local supporters welcomed the arrival of Tessa and her orange-clad band on the little plateau on the western slope. With amazing alacrity, the former compound prisoners now reversed roles with their erstwhile captors, dramatically accelerating the process of tying up commandos with whatever materials the scrub, or the train wreck, could furnish.

The point had soon been reached where Constable Baker felt confident enough to temporarily leave the scene, moving off briskly toward a distant farmhouse in order to telephone the Commonwealth authorities and defence forces. Behind him, meanwhile, a still sneering Inspector Jensen continued to hurl insults.

'Boy scout! You haven't heard the last o' this. Some of my cobbers'll sort you out. Your career's over, ya little scumbag.'

Young Baker did not deign so much as to turn his head: his reply was instead a laconic finger, angled skywards above his shoulder. By contrast, a red-faced Jemima Blackman, hands still securely tied, had plenty to say.

'What a crummy coalition,' she screeched. 'A mob of bush woops, a Lady Bountiful lawyer and an egghead professor. Well, you'll never make any of this stick. We've got too many connections. We'll ruin the lot of you. As for you, Bainbridge, you should have stayed back in the hallowed halls and ivory towers.' She turned her leonine gaze full on Hugh now, and her eyes flamed like sapphires.

'You could have wasted the exchequer's mouldy old reserves there for years, like your kind have always done. There's no room for your old order out here – or anywhere else for that matter. Your antiquated traditions and values are finished.'

'Well, well; so this is *la belle dame sans merci*, is it?' Hugh smiled. 'All set to *outscold the ranting actor on the stage* by the sound of it, if we'll forgive a little mixing of quotations. Well, let me simply say, madam, that unlike you I'm in the company of honourable people – people I'm proud to know, and to call friends.'

Jemima tossed her blonde mane, shooting Hugh a sardonic sideways glance. 'Well, perhaps it's not so surprising after all. They do say that poetry is the literature of barbarians: unlike the works of the scientists and the rational economists, whose writings will actually benefit society for years to come.'

'Oh dear; another person who's misread Peacock.' Hugh stared back at the woman. 'You'll forgive me – I'm not one to gloat, but I venture to suggest that the very worst poetry will prove to be both more enduring, and of more benefit to society, than your recent misuse of science and economic doctrine.'

For around half an hour, Jemima, Inspector Jensen and several of the commandos continued to jeer and threaten their captors, issuing dire warnings about a wave of retribution which would follow their inevitable release, until at last the tension was broken by the rhythmic beat of helicopter blades and the wail of police sirens. Constable Ben Baker rushed up, panting, in time to welcome and give directions to a veritable sea of blue uniforms, which now came swirling up the slopes of Cattle Mountain.

This Queensland police contingent quickly converged with a swarm of figures in black riot gear, who had been disgorged by the choppers on a couple of clear plateaux higher up; and now the private citizens who had been instrumental in thwarting a dangerous coup could relax and cheerfully relinquish their responsibilities.

Arm in arm, Tessa and Hugh ambled down the western slopes, following a convoy made up of the Steiler brothers, their more resolute neighbours and the orange clad folk who had so recently been prisoners on the other side of the mountain. It was Wally Steiler who appeared to best sum up the prevailing mood. 'Motley lookin' lot, aren't we?' he suggested in a casual, light-hearted tone. 'To have such a big job come our way?'

Hugh paused for a moment beside the slain *Diablo*, gazing quietly at the bulbous contours of the vast wreck. 'A *'rough beast'* that one, Muffet,' he said at length. 'To *'come slouching forth'*.'

'Yes.' Tess was also in pensive mood. 'It's almost certain that the *centre* would not have held, if that beast – and its message – had been *'loosed upon the world'*.'

'We all owe you a very great debt, Tessa,' the professor said, his voice betraying unusual emotion. 'A great debt.'

Tess looked a little embarrassed. 'What about you, Hugh? And all these people? I don't really think I did all that much.'

'You were the one who first went out on a limb, Muffet. And you've been out there ever since. The quality that shines through is pure selflessness: the risks were all taken for the good of others, not for yourself.'

'I seem to remember that you also went out on a limb, Hugh.' The lawyer smiled.

'Yes – until the confounded thing broke. Enough said perhaps.' Hugh took her arm again and they walked off quickly in the tracks of the Steiler brothers, who were calling back an invitation.

'Hurry up, you blokes,' Wally shouted. 'Emil reckons he's got the makin's of a batch o' pikelets back at the house – and I'll be puttin' the kettle on for a brew o' tea as soon as I get inside the flamin' door. After all that exercise, a man's bloody near starvin', eh?'

Chapter Twenty-One
Saturday 23rd July 1977 – 7pm

A WESTERLY WIND WAS again blowing, but the occupants of the little lean-to in the hills appeared unperturbed. Dressed warmly against the cold, huddling close to the fire as friendly bubbles rippled the water in their billy, they sat and watched while an honest, cheery moon arced up from the ridges.

'So when do you think you'll head home, Hugh?' Tessa leaned back comfortably in the professor's arms, her silky brown hair soft against his jaw.

'Well, no real rush,' he said, his tone suggesting that he was certainly in no hurry to go anywhere. 'I suppose I should soon make contact with my co-researcher on the bush poets project, and I imagine you'll want to get back to Sydney, and your work, fairly soon.'

'Actually, this probably sounds a bit naughty,' she said softly. 'But right now I wish it would rain. Rain hard, enough to bring the creek down a banker, so that we'd be stranded up here for a few days – or weeks.'

'Hmm. Now that's an inviting prospect. Mind you, Muffet, we would probably miss our careers, if we didn't have them. And I will be back out here again very shortly, you know – to give evidence at the trial of that nefarious lot.'

'Mmm. That's good then. From what I know of

criminal law – though it's not my area of course – you'll be able to supply a certain amount of evidence in written form, to assist the crown in building its case, but you'll certainly be needed in person when it goes to trial.'

'I'll be there. And it will take a lot more than their hollow threats to stop me – which leads me to wonder, in fact, just how extensive their support network really is, or was.'

'It's probably more a case of "was",' Tessa suggested. 'I could imagine that a lot of peripheral and lukewarm supporters will soon develop very cold feet, once the full facts start to be aired, particularly when they realise the sheer degree of evil involved, and when they see the ringleaders brought to trial. A few more rotten apples may be discovered in the process, which will be all to the good.'

'Indeed. Amazing, isn't it, how otherwise talented people – Arblaster with his engineering expertise; Ms Blackman with her business acumen – could choose to direct their considerable skills against the common weal?'

'It certainly is. I suppose we all like to think that there's a vast gulf between the idealist and the zealot; between those who believe in a certain philosophy and those who want to impose it on others; but some people seem to make the jump, from enthusiast to extremist, so easily. What did your Mr Wyatt think, when you phoned him from the Junction Ridge post office?'

'He seemed more than a little surprised at the turn of events out here,' Hugh chuckled. 'Though he'd always had Arblaster pegged as a nutter, based purely on his correspondence. From my description of the Diablo's hovering technology, he doesn't rate its chances highly as a viable future transport system either. "Too much fuel would be required for too little benefit", I believe he said – hullo then! Who's this? Someone coming our way with a flashlight.'

The bobbing beam of an Eveready 'Big Jim' was indeed playing along one of the game trails which led up the hillside toward the lean-to.

'Who's there?' Hugh demanded.

'I thought you blokes might have the billy on,' came a cheery voice, as two male figures materialised in the moonlit clearing.

'Wally, old chap,' beamed the professor. 'And Emil. Come and have a cup of tea and warm yourselves by the fire. It's good to see you, but isn't it a bit cool for an evening stroll.'

'Well, we weren't sure when you blokes were leavin',' said Wally. 'And we wanted to catch up before you shot through back to the big smoke. The old ute won't get up the track this far – not like that Land Rover you're drivin' – so we thought bugger it, we'll come on Shanks' pony.'

'Oh, we were planning to come and see you before we left,' Tessa reassured the brothers. 'You can't get rid of us that easily.'

'Nah, that'd be right,' Emil joked. 'Well, the walk'll do us good; an' the wind's droppin' now. Did you get your shotgun back?'

'Yes thanks,' Tess said. 'We walked back over on Wednesday afternoon, after everything had settled down, and got it out of the tree. I've cleaned and oiled it, and it's back in its case.'

'Good girl,' Wally said. 'Now the truth is, we've come to fetch you a little something to take home, both of you. O' course, these things are a bit rough, but maybe you can stick 'em up at home somewhere: if not, just use 'em for firewood.'

From out of a hessian bag, Wally and Emil now extracted two wall plates, fashioned with exquisite care from the fallen branches of an ironbark tree. Hugh and Tessa took the gifts and read aloud the inscriptions, which were the same on each.

From quiet homes and first beginning.
Out to the undiscovered ends.
There's nothing worth the wear of winning.
But laughter and the love of friends.
Hilaire Belloc

'Got the verse from a book my old school-teacher gave me,' Wally explained. 'Reckoned you'd know the lines – anyway, hope you like 'em.'

'I shall treasure this,' said Hugh, with a slight quaver in his voice. He shook the hands of both brothers warmly.

'Me too.' Tessa Scott, eyes glistening, gave each of the bushmen a long hug and a kiss on the cheek. 'I know just the place at the townhouse for this – just above the front door.'

The tea had brewed and was soon doing its warming, cheering work around the campfire, while easy conversation flowed and the benevolent moon rode through a cavalcade of brilliant if lesser lights across a cloudless sky; till at last it was time to say goodnight and the brothers, in jocular mood, trundled off with their flashlight down the track.

Behind them, again in each other's embrace, the lawyer and the professor gazed up at the blazing stars and the almost palpable quiet of the evening.

'The extreme rationalists, the cynical technocrats, the Jemimas and Arblasters; they're all missing out on so many things, aren't they?' It was Tessa who first broke the silence, followed by a chorus of bovine utterances down in the gully. 'Their only yardstick seems to be utility – little else, nothing for balance. Perhaps they really need to pause awhile – how does William Henry Davies put it?

What is this life if, full of care,
We have no time to stand and stare?'

Hugh glanced up at an overhanging eucalypt, glistening silver in the moonlight.

'No time to stand beneath the boughs
And stare as long as sheep or cows.'
'No time to see, in broad daylight,' Tessa whispered.

They were skipping passages now, but it did not seem to matter. *'Streams full of stars, like skies at night.'*

'No time to turn at Beauty's glance,' Hugh was speaking softly also, his gaze now directed only at Tess. *'And watch her feet, how they can dance.'* Her eyes and face were to him a vision of loveliness, radiant in the moonglow.

No time to wait, till her mouth can
Enrich that smile her eyes began.'

And gently and softly they kissed.

SOMETIME DURING THE night Tessa and Hugh awoke to the gentle sound of raindrops on the lean-to's corrugated iron roof. Where had that come from? The early night had been crystal clear, yet soon the rain was bucketing down, its runoff plunging down the gullies in torrents. They might just possibly get the Land Rover down the hillside, but the Fiat – never.

They were stranded.

Post Script

MANY READERS MAY wonder why the technology of the steam powered hover train has not been taken up, and perhaps even improved upon, in the thirty odd years since the events in the foregoing narrative took place. After all, the idea of a vehicle that can transport large numbers of people across virtually any terrain, without tracks or formed roads, is certainly an attractive one. The answer to this mystery was hinted at by James Wyatt, during the intercontinental phone call which Hugh instigated from the Junction Ridge Post Office on 23rd July 1977 – in a word, economics.

During the eighties, the same business principles which the inventor of the *Diablo* claimed to follow (though *he* took them to criminal extremes) were observed and applied by a series of interested investors, who carefully evaluated the train's feasibility as a means of mass transit. The overwhelming consensus was that too much fuel would be needed for too little financial return, given the number of people who might be expected to use such a hover train service.

Other seemingly insurmountable hurdles lay in gaining sufficient access to private and public property to liberate the system from conventional track corridors, superficially one of its most desirable features. In the long run, too many practical engineering and economic factors mitigated against the adoption and further refinement of the *Diablo's* technology. While the development of hover trains has continued apace, using ideas such as linear induction motors and the Maglev concept (a magnetic-powered, levitating train), the notion of combining steam propulsion with hovering capability has – if the reader will pardon a truly outrageous pun – never made it off the ground.

In setting the record straight, it should be noted that one particular feature of one of Arblaster's contrivances has found a measure of acceptance. While clearly he did not invent the retractable stadium dome so common around the world today, his membranous covering for the *Diablo's* crater was possibly the first roof over such a large area to feature an organic surface with natural grass. In 1991, a flock of about 100 sheep grazed on the now iconic (though firmly fixed) roof of Australia's Parliament House, just as cattle and wallabies no doubt did on Arblaster's sliding and folding structure. Most people will find it hard to pay such a megalomaniac too much credit for thinking up the idea of a large grassed roof, however, when his underlying aims, and those of his cohorts, were so clearly anti-social *and* anti-environmental.

Many will also wonder what happened to the vast network of supporters claimed by the Blackman/Arblaster/Jensen triumvirate. Like the *Diablo's* steam technology, this menacing spectre also appeared to dissipate and drift away. Certainly some corruption was uncovered within the ranks of the Queensland police service (and the forces of other states), but the individuals involved were, and are, far outnumbered by officers of exemplary standards – in short, those who adhere to the ethics and principles of constable Ben Baker clearly won the day over the followers of Inspector Jensen.

In similar fashion, a handful of high-flying business moguls, a smattering of company executives, some minor political figures and even a few farmers were arrested and convicted, following the successful prosecution of the *Diablo* project's ringleaders and their mercenary pack; it must be said, however, that most of the people originally attracted to Jemima Blackman's ideas were quickly disillusioned when the full extent of her ruthless methods was made public during and after her trial.

It has been suggested that a few original supporters of the *Diablo* project might have subsequently modified their extremist tendencies sufficiently to allow them to drift into conventional or mainstream political parties: if so, we should all be vigilant; and beware extremist rhetoric whenever and wherever it may surface.

Acknowledgments

MOONLIGHT EXPRESS has been a labour of love for some considerable time, inspired by the country where I grew up and places I regularly visit. It could never have seen the light of day, however, without the assistance of some fabulous people. I am especially indebted to John Cokley of *Strictly Literary*, for his guidance, encouragement and fantastic support over many years. Academic, columnist, literary agent and publisher *par excellence*, John has worked tirelessly and selflessly to discover, nurture and motivate writers across Australia and to launch their work into the global marketplace.

I am grateful to several people who took the time and trouble to read early drafts of the manuscript, providing much-needed objectivity and advice in their feedback. In particular, thanks are due to Anna Kassulke, Lynne Alsop, Karin Toovey, Emma Green, Irena Thomson, Rae Webb, Mel Jones, Jim Corkery, Katie Davies, Rachel Lethem and Desley Greensill. All their comments and assessments have been invaluable to the end product. Thanks also – with much love – to Pauline, Emma and Luke, for being who they are and putting up with my eccentricities.

Geoff Barlow
April 2012

www.ingramcontent.com/pod-product-compliance
Lightning Source LLC
LaVergne TN
LVHW020708110826
845149LV00012B/2158

9780987086587